David Hughes was born in Hampshire in 1930 and educated at King's College School, Wimbledon and Christ Church, Oxford, where he read English. He is currently fiction reviewer for the *Mail on Sunday*. His better-known novels include *The Major*, *Memories of Dying*, *The Imperial German Dinner Service* and *The Pork Butcher*. Amongst his works of non-fiction are *A Study of J. B. Priestl*[illegible] travel book, *The Road to Stockholm*. David Hughes lives [illegible] is wife and their two small children.

DAVID HUGHES

The Imperial German Dinner Service

PALADIN
GRAFTON BOOKS
A Division of the Collins Publishing Group

LONDON GLASGOW
TORONTO SYDNEY AUCKLAND

Paladin
Grafton Books
A Division of the Collins Publishing Group
8 Grafton Street, London W1X 3LA

Published in Paladin Books 1987

First published in Great Britain by
Constable & Co Ltd 1983

ISBN 0-586-08575-0

Printed and bound in Great Britain by
Collins, Glasgow

Set in Plantin

To Whom It May Concern

I'm all right, but I'm redundant. A spoilt, angry, bored and aimless reporter is what I am. If not recession, it was probably too many adjectives or drinks that got me the push. One hates working, but not working's worse.

My wife Sophie is also all right. A spoilt, well-off, beautiful and busy journalist, who runs the Arts Diary in one of the Sundays and is unfaithful. A working woman.

A year ago Sophie bought a derelict cottage in Hampshire. Her scheme was for me to run up a do-it-yourself paradise for her – to give me an interest. But I don't like doing it myself. So she started going down alone every weekend to reduce the place to order, while I went on brooding in town.

Her floorboards were not only rotten, but encrusted with dried excrement. An old chap called Fentiman had kept all his cats shut indoors for company. Thanks to charitable neighbours, he had been led away by male nurses to an old people's home.

When Sophie began jemmying up the floorboards she found an embroidered bag tied with string and a dish wrapped in a newspaper from 1940. The bag contained a dozen sovereigns. She shared this buried treasure with no one. The dish, for want of a newsier subject, she popped into her column as a tailpiece.

Sophie's method in this column (my idea) was to hold up a mirror to her own mediocrity, feign ignorance of art, and nudge the readership for advice. It made things lively. Know-alls wrote in correcting her facts. Busybodies put her taste to rights.

To keep this lot guessing, Sophie described the olive tints that washed in and out of the vine-leaves round the dish's rim.

Also the glazed drawing of a country mansion on its centre got the kind of coy exposure her style favoured.

Where was this place? And of what period? On the back of the dish – so she said – time had rubbed out the maker's name. It hadn't. She could read it quite clearly.

It said Wedgwood.

It also said 1914, and she didn't announce that either.

Sharpening the mystery, she then mentioned the symbol that interrupted the garland of vine-leaves. An eagle. A grand formalised sort of eagle. Quote elegantly belligerent unquote – that was her phrase for it.

The mansion looked English enough in its surround of parkland. But the eagle? Readers please identify. A bottle of good hock was on offer for the best answer.

Sophie hadn't bothered to phone the publicity chaps at Barlaston. Wedgwoods could have told her what she had found.

So could I. But she didn't ask. In any case I usually deflect her questions. She doesn't like truth.

Only a few days earlier it had happened. I was busy killing time – okay, 'researching' a freelance story nobody would buy, about antiques – one wet morning in Bournemouth. Even less okay, I was chatting up one of the stand-bys of my tedium, a widow of jaded charms called Myra Tremlett. As a girl she had known Augustus John and now she was selling classy junk. Need I say more to give you the cultural effect? At forty she was still amply nubile, though I had known her for years.

'Oh, Mr Patcham,' she said, all arch.

'Something up your sleeve for me, Mrs Tremlett?'

On a story like this, on any story, any evidence will do. And the piece she showed me now was a gravy-boat.

'It's a sauce-tureen, Roland,' she said.

On one flank this object – later confirmed as vintage dinner service – bore the image of a structure I knew well.

I had been married in it.

It was a Norman church tucked under the breast of a Dorset hill on the outskirts of a village called West Dole. A Romanesque showpiece, according to Pevsner. It was overhung by sheer coppices which even during weddings – and not much else happened there, except funerals – thickened the light inside the church into the grain on a photograph.

Even in reality it looked badly reproduced on newsprint. Here on the pot it resembled an artist's impression. Which is what it was.

But I rather liked the piece. I didn't care much for its associations. I liked the feel of it in my hands. It felt like power. I could do nasty things to Sophie with it, not hit her, but hurt her.

Sophie Singer married me there at the end of 1966. And M. Tremlett knew this, hence the offer. Sophie's present lover, Courtney Ranston, had been my best man. He was now Director of National Arts. I decided our nuptial church on a gravy-boat was a tender present to bring back to Sophie or – if that were possible – it probably wasn't – bring her back to me. And Myra's shadowed eye, almost a wink, confirmed the romantic cruelty of facing Sophie with an image of her vows.

I got home to Boxer Road, SW8, with the tureen wrapped in paper. By now I felt proud of the gift, hoping supper would be ready. Chili con carne perhaps, even pasta.

Sophie was out, however. There was the silence to prove it, but also the usual gratuitous note. Which said nothing. She had got me up (or got me in) some sandwiches – which meant guilt, in other words a night with Ranston. I could have had better sandwiches on the train.

I put the wrapped tureen carefully on the table among the coffee mugs, review books, broken recorders, package brochures, invites to openings, clutter, bric-a-brac and her cuttings. Then, while I was opening some Côtes-du-Something, the bottle slipped, banged hard on the stripped pine, jiggled for a moment like a skittle, and rolled away splashing wine in bloody swathes across Sophie's chaos.

The paper went suddenly crimson.

The tureeen whizzed off the table, to drop with a rumbling thud on the lino.

I looked with control at the sandwiches.

As usual they were filled with a meat not on my list of favourites. Sophie liked to tease.

Then I stood, the bottle still glugging over a last week's *Standard*. And picked up the pieces.

Sophie Singer. I fell for the name – I mean, the hiss of it. It had sounded like a sweet nothing. The marriage is a bit of a whisper these days too.

Seventeen years old it is. And she's still only 35. I'm a good 50, if good's the word. She had just picked up three A-levels at a school in Dorset when I picked her up at a club in Camden Town. It was battle royal at first sight.

I'm short and squat and dumpy in the middle and sinewy at the extremities. I'm pleased with my body – its obstinacy, the way it has stood the test of time.

At least I'm not bald. I have that wiry hair in coils that makes women think of babies. And big lustrous eyes that make them think of the activities that lead to babies. I've had a good run for my money. But never any money.

We live in our own house in Stockwell.

It's not our house at all. For one thing it's in Sophie's name, due to a sentimental error on my part. Also there's a crone, due for demolition when we moved in, who has soldiered on lousing up the top floor for the last fifteen years.

In the basement lives a 'student'. So-called male. If he were not as gay as a church social, he would constitute a threat to domestic bliss. But anything is a threat to domestic bliss. This man throws the sort of party where even the women come dressed as women. Once he brought in a lemur which electrocuted itself on a faulty fitting which for months Terence had been asking me to repair.

The house, as stated, is in Boxer Road, SW8. The late Boxer was a local alderman who had the privilege of laying a foundation stone of a hostel for the under-privileged. Those were the golden days when people round here were just poor. Now they're also in a mess. They're out of work, angry, spoilt, bored, aimless and often black, and have dozens of children.

But Sophie and I are not staying together for the sake of the children. We have no children. There was one who died. It was his death that delayed me mending the fault that saw off the lemur. In the midst of life, we are in Boxer Road. Sophie and I are together because we hate our shared knowledge that we love liking each other. I can put it no better.

Enough of this, Patcham. On with the story.

The church at West Dole wasn't too badly smashed on the lino. A dozen bits or so. The roof was cleft in twain, as by lightning. The north porch – I remember the wedding pix outside it – had suffered damage.

But being redundant nags you. With anxiety I started reading into this petty disaster things that weren't there. Never had been there. Probably wouldn't be.

After all, the drawing had been done long before we married. This, in ruins, was the church at West Dole as it was in 1914 or thereabouts. I wasn't born then. I had no responsibility for it.

Other thoughts followed in this muddy wake. Was it because we had never had children, or rather had lost one, that Sophie was now out gallivanting? A jagged break occurred in the tureen where, as best man, Courtney Ranston had stood ogling the camera, already on the brink of going public. Even then fame was his pair of spurs.

They would now be in bed. She always whimpered to excess

in moments of sexual triumph. But I no longer had much say in that either. She was her own mistress, apart from being his. And they both had jobs.

After a bite of the derisive sandwiches I laid out the bits and pieces of 1914 on the corner of the table. Down in the basement Terence was in, plying an off-duty mugger with hash. He lent me some glue, but not for sniffing – the real stuff, for sticking things together.

And then, for an hour, for hours, I concentrated. For me this was quite a change.

I focused on the absolute necessity of making good the damage. No conscious thought here. I just wanted to bring back to perfection what I had destroyed by chance.

But also I was exploiting that concentration to blot out the unthinkable evening in Ranston's place in Chelsea, then dinner, a bloody good dinner somewhere, wine less obvious than my Domaine-de-Whatsit, and between them that calm sense of things not being broken, not needing to be edged into place with tweezers and glue.

At one moment the church porch, where we had stood grinning at the future, slipped, and I had to start from scratch. I longed for a hammer to smash the lot. But with patience I kept at work, like piecing together memory.

And when I finished it it seemed to mean nothing. I had merely done it. It didn't speak volumes. It only asked to be left to dry.

The evening was half over. I had spent hours fiddling and soon with any luck Sophie would come back smelling of after-shave.

And I might feel secure.

Next day I woke up (alone) obsessed by the object I had repaired. So I kept it a secret from Sophie. She came in dewily fulfilled at breakfast time, as if Chelsea were a noted health-farm.

Our convention required her to say that she had been out dancing all night or an aunt was ill or the arts editor had kept her up late and she had kipped down on the office floor. This time she said nothing and smelt of bubble-bath.

But in my black heart I made the most of the little present I'd decided not to give her. She had secrets, okay, fine. I had one of my own in that tureen. At least it had a past, even if I lacked a future.

I would use it ruthlessly when the time was ripe.

Sophie changed. (I would finger her cast-offs for clues as soon as she left.) As a sop to me she then rang up an aunt to make sure she was well and truly ill. Two more cooling mugs of coffee got pushed into the debris on the table. Then she phoned the arts editor to agree to work late. (All I wanted was to hug her.) Then, thank goodness, she went out to chase up some story about a new sculpture that would turn the working-classes into instant aesthetes.

She is very beautiful, my Sophie. I know that because I am very jealous. I prefer it when she is not there, while detesting her absence.

Alone at last, I called the Wedgwood factory near Stoke-on-Trent. And got hold of some lackey in the sales department. From my description he said that what I had probably bought, in all ignorance, then broken, was part of the Imperial German Dinner Service.

The what?

'The Imperial German Dinner Service,' the man said patiently.

This grand set consisted of over a thousand pieces in all, which Wedgwoods had been commissioned to make for the Kaiser just before the Great War. Pieces popped up now and again, but not often. Every item had been unique. Whether serving-dish, fruit-bowl, side-plate, ladle or indeed sauce-tureen, each bore a different picture of the England of that era. These ranged from cathedrals through sea-shores to village streets and back again via stately homes to the great landmarks of the capital.

By all accounts, said my man in the Potteries, the whole had been a masterpiece. Little remained in this country but sketches and a few 'seconds' – and of course bills which the Kaiser, for reasons not hard to find, had never footed.

Holding the phone I thought: Christ, how exciting! The old feeling: a story; exclusive – just me *v.* the rest.

Why had the Imperial German Dinner Service vanished?

I was drily told that an awful lot had happened in Europe and to Europe during the last 70 years. Crockery, as I had just proved, was fragile. Yes, if I brought the piece north, they would be happy to inspect and identify it. Certainly I could look at a few relics in their museum.

As for the church at West Dole, the directors might possibly have made me a modest offer for it.

How modest an offer?

Well, the fellow couldn't commit the Board to more than a hundred pounds, always assuming the piece to be perfect. Which we both knew it wasn't.

But again this excitement! Think of it – in an almost scornful way a value had been established. At rock-bottom prices, quoted at random by an underling on the telephone, the entire Service was worth nothing short of a hundred thousand pounds.

So where was it?

Back from her flirtation with high-rise sculpture, Sophie caught me not exactly napping, but planning what to do next.

'What have you been up to, darling?'

Nowadays Sophie never asked me what I had been up to, lest I reply with the same question. We were not bored with each other's activities. I was afraid of hers and she was scared of hearing about my lack of any of my own.

'Why this sudden interest?'

'You look changed,' Sophie said, head cocked. 'What are you taking for it?'

'Taking?'

'Haven't you been to a doctor? You're suffering from rude health, Roland. A glitter in the eye.'

'I just thought I'd alter my system.'

'Have you got one left? I thought hypochondriacs were convinced their systems had been destroyed.'

She had the knack of making me sound heavy going even to myself. I said pettishly, 'I'm talking about my old system of wasting my life.'

'Oh, darling, why change a work of art? We all admire it very much.' She also had a dread trick of seeming to mean what she said. 'It's quite unique, you know. It involves using everything for the wrong purpose. Most people get out of bed in the morning. Not you. You "plan the day" in it. Then you don't read papers or eat toast like normal mortals – you spin them out to propel you towards drinks. And that's when life begins to seem just a tiny bit more lifelike to you. But, darling, it's been life since the crack of dawn – being so busy planning, you've missed it!'

None of this had the bite of insult. Indeed it sounded almost fond. Sophie needed to seem to care, so that her vulnerable duplicity would never be threatened by a false move on her part. She called it manners. Oddly enough I myself had no wish to shatter these formalities. I needed Sophie's infidelity just as much as she did; it kept my sex taut and angry, if to no purpose.

'So why are we tolerating all this?' I said, riskily passing to the offensive.

'All what?' Sophie looked round in bewilderment, as if the mess she lived in had suddenly cleared up.

'Want a drink?'

'Now you're talking.'

After her third vodka gimlet, or whatever, she would almost think herself half in love with me. I now mixed her first one. It was a screwdriver. She was always trying funny cocktails culled from the thrillers she pretended to read for work. Background, she called it. I passed her the drink icily, then said, 'If you're accusing me of avoiding life, we're all the same. The only times I've ever enjoyed the bloody thing was when I was getting myself ready to live it.'

'Despair not,' Sophie said. 'You'll get your chance again.'

'Working for newspapers doesn't count. That's also a way of waiting for something to happen. And it never does.'

'Lovely drink,' Sophie said, sipping.

'Are you any better at it? I'm middle-aged, Sophie. I still feel I'm equipping myself for the mark I'm supposed to make on the world – later, always later. My whole life is spent deciding what to do, not doing it.'

'Doesn't that sound rather immature, even to you?'

'Yes. You should be treating me as a student.'

'Oh, precious, you really are in a bad way.' She held her glass at arm's length for a refill. 'Perhaps I was right about you seeing a doctor – you know, the *real* sort.' She tapped her head.

'I wonder what my old friend Courtney thinks about it all.'

'God, give me that drink quickly,' Sophie said. 'I'd rather hit the bottle than you.'

'It was only a question – you know, those things that journalists ask.'

'You've no right to intrude on my privacy. You're only a student.'

'Yes. I'm learning fast.'

'Why aren't you being funny? You used to amuse your friends.'

And then all at once, with a stupid sense of being alone, I didn't want to tell Sophie anything any more. The jokes were over. I had been taking all this trouble to make an opening to share my interest in the Dinner Service with her. Now I closed down. It actually felt like a door shutting in my body, a not quite audible snap.

Her attack on me didn't matter a hoot. I was used to this material, if in less aggressive form.

But now I was no longer intrigued by her reasons for going on at me. I wasn't even working up, after her third cocktail, then dinner, a bit of wine, to making love to her, in darkness, as to another man's woman.

One was never lonely with the thought of revenge. But now even that faded from me.

I didn't want her elegance – her neat way of turning not only debating-points but my very thoughts against me – above all her self-deception that had conditioned me to think it my own.

I simply wanted a breath of fresh air.

'Are you off?' she said, surprised, holding an empty glass.

'Yes.' Then savagely: 'See you some time.'

Driven by annoyance, I drove to West Dole. In her car. It took three hours.

I had avoided the church for years. There, after all, I had committed an act of faith to a woman that had produced, instead of passion, not even routine.

Now I was on my own. Rain swirled locally. Far away last glints of the sun pocked the downs.

I hurried into the porch for shelter and stood breathing hard, looking out at the yew-lined path where bulbs had flashed on that remote day of my wedding. A few notices flapped on the board. A parochial election was due.

In fact I dreaded turning my back on the weather to enter the church. The interior loomed like a dimension well beyond the limits of the picture I had of myself.

I had a lighter, which flicked on and off, burning my fingers. Memorial plaques flared, every syllable on the damp walls predicating a world that had ended in 1914. Victorians of the district massed their sensible lives into brief marbled obituary. The seventeenth century presented its compliments to death in golden Latin.

There existed not a murmur of my own times. My feet clanged up the gratings where old heating-systems were entrenched, and as I looked at the glimmer of a cross on the altar, there arose in me, pat, the excitement which I'd been trying to play down ever since this very building came into focus for me that wet morning in Bournemouth.

I tried to locate the feeling. It was as sidelong as happiness. What did the church mean? Well, it meant that I could soon be making money out of its image on the sauce-boat – that hundred smackers quoted by the chap at Wedgwoods could be only a starting price. Each piece, if I could find it, might be worth up to a thousand. The search had just to start with a measure of luck to finance its own progress.

My efforts would improve the rarity of the Dinner Service; items in known possession would suddenly be valued at far more than their true worth; I could create a market in the unique. But most of all, and at last, I would be selling myself, at my own estimate of proper value, to a world that had sacked me.

There was also the mystery. Neither I nor anyone else knew for sure where the Dinner Service was. The notion of a fragile England, manufactured in a substance intended for practical daily use, but now, thanks to the quiddities of history, scattered all over the place, or perhaps not existing at all except as a memory, filled my spirits in that church with exactly the kind of challenge which I had spent my life failing – or, rather, failing to find.

The stained glass dimmed. My eyes were getting used to the gloom. I felt immured in a world which had to all appearances gone for good – though still reflected on the artifact I had repaired. A world representing values which only I had miraculously had the sense to think of pursuing and preserving and bringing back. The whole thing existed somewhere. I had the power – the inclination at any rate – to find it.

I walked back in the dusk to my car with an exuberance I had lacked for years. This preposterous feeling lasted no time at all.

But I remembered it. When I got home Sophie was sitting up in bed in a scarlet kimono designed in East Sussex by a drop-out factory manager's wife who kept sheep, scribbling away at her piece for next Sunday.

'The power of the press,' she said with a genial sigh. 'It just comes gushing out of me.'

It seemed a good moment to broach my future.

'I liked your bit about that plate, Sophie.'

'What plate? Oh, yes, that.'

'I wanted to talk to you about it.'

'Everyone's talking to me about it,' Sophie said. 'Even the Prince. Why don't you talk to me about something else? Don't be shy.'

'The Prince?'

'Well, darling, one of the Princes, I can't rightly remember which.'

'How did he get wind of it?'

'Wind of what?'

'The plate.'

'He reads me, doesn't he?' Sophie said. 'He reads me like a book. I'm his culture pulse. He takes me thrice daily on Sundays. He can't live without me – no, but in fact he was opening this mini-expo on the South Bank last week, and I was lined up to meet him – curtsey, grin, blush – and they're jolly well briefed, you know, because in a trice he'd won my bottle of hock. It's the Imperial German Dinner Service, says he.'

'Why the hell would he know a thing like that?'

'Didn't it belong to his great-grandfather's mother's son-in-law's nephew or something? Anyway these royals are so inbred they think everything belongs to them. He said how British it was and how sad that we as a nation don't know our art from our elbow or words to that effect.' She paused with a reminiscent smirk over her brush with the mighty. 'And I've had a postbag as fat as your tumtum – you must lose weight, darling – from all the usual idiots claiming to be experts. It's quite a story.'

I liked none of this, and it showed. Sophie glanced at me, suspicious but a bit bored, bound as a journalist to assume ulterior motives. 'What's your interest?'

'I've decided to look for it.'

'For what? What for?'

'The Dinner Service.'

'I wouldn't bother,' she said quickly. 'It's in hand.'

'What does that mean?'

'Don't ask me,' Sophie said. 'I just do vaguely know that some conspiracy's going on. In any case you're not the first on the trail.'

'Who is, Sophie?'

'Oh, you are a bully . . . I had this letter from some doctor – why go on about it? – you know, the one who looked after Mr Fentiman, who sweetly sold me his cottage. He got it into his head that the IGDS – that's what we cognos call it for short – was part of the national heritage and the Krauts ought to have posted it back to us at the Treaty of Versailles.' Sophie drew a tired breath. 'That sort of guff. So he spent his little all toddling round Europe looking for the goods.'

'Have you tried to see him?'

'Certainly.'

'What did he say?'

'Nothing.'

'Is it so secret?'

'No,' Sophie said. 'He's dead.'

We looked at each other with a sort of ironic pity, as if Fentiman's death had a bearing on our lives that ought to mean something.

'Did he find the Dinner Service?'

'All I know is he wrote up his search for it, tried to get it published. Bad timing – 1939, war broke out. No dice.'

'What happened to his papers?'

'He shoved them into some archive in his will.'

'Where?'

'Can't say, darling. All the facts belong to my newspaper.'

'That's never stopped a reporter helping a friend. Or even an enemy.'

'You know I can't leak sources.'

'Would you for money?' I said nastily.

'No, because you couldn't pay enough.' At once, in her silly home-counties kimono, she looked ashamed. 'Don't get involved, Roland,' she said. Then: 'All right – it's Winchester.' A frown. 'But you can't win.'

'Try me,' I said.

Taking the museum steps two at a time, bumping at the top into a tourist – this lack of condition was dreadful – I entered a lofty vestibule solemnified by glass cases of blunt nails, arrowheads and stuff. Here, puffed out, I asked a muted clerk for the Director.

Bureaucracy reared. My name and business were inscribed, as if at arm's length, on a form for visitors. My toes tensed with impatience.

At that moment a dishevelled man in baggy corduroys jogged down the staircase. He looked at me sidelong with a lunatic grin, then said in thin metallic tones that echoed back an Oxford of long ago, 'Hullo – you here, Roland? How strange, yes, but how strangely inevitable things look and feel as the years pass. Jung, doesn't he, calls it synchronicity?'

A hollow groan formed inside, dipping me in the shallows of youth again. Not for a quarter of a century had I listened to the effusions of Desmond Turvey's disordered brains.

He had lived above me – above himself, for that matter – on the same staircase at Univ. He was always hovering lankily in my rooms, spilling the insides of sandwiches on to my furniture and exposing the banality of other people's thought.

How the silly bugger had talked! He had also taken out punting a girl favoured by me, put her through impenetrable jungles of philosophy fringed by willows, then seduced her to the frenzied slap of water on the planks.

But now: 'Desmond!' I cried with involuntary glee.

In clothes worn like mannerisms, in his tattered turns of phrase, Turvey was the whole of my Oxford to the seedy core. He looked unchanged and, still worse, unbeaten. He had always made a point of lacking reality.

'Didn't know you were researching here,' he went on, 'or we'd have lunched more often, nice little wine-place just opened, quite civilised for Alfred's capital, no burnt cakes.'

Why the devil should I be researching anywhere? The clown was making assumptions, as he always had. So blinkered by persistent adolescence that he could see others only as projections of himself – though of lesser weight.

'They've put me in charge – what can one do? – of the museums here,' he said, implying with sorry patronage that my application for the post had failed. 'You'll have been marking the changes. So odd we haven't run across each other. Was it Froude, or perhaps Macaulay, you remember, who considered Winchester the true heart of the country?'

'You tell me, Desmond,' I said without grace.

'You may have noticed London is coming round to this view of Winchester,' Turvey said. 'Only yesterday I was rung up by Courtney Ranston, the National Arts supremo. You possibly don't know him unless you've been popping up to town recently, but he's beginning to move things on the Arts scene – and move them in the right direction, we all think.'

We all? All I felt now, and quite enough, was a giddy suspicion of paranoia.

'What did he want, Desmond?'

'A good question.' His eyes, underhung by smudges of midnight oil, blinked evasively. 'Well, he has asked me, if not in so many words, as it were, to put together an exhibition for him,' Turvey said, again with the hint that I had missed this chance by a whisker. 'Have you a moment before you go back to your desk?'

'What desk, Desmond?'

'I'll show you, then. I've been holing up here overnight reading through the papers.'

'Which papers, Desmond?'

He gestured vaguely with grubby fingers. Of course I knew which papers.

I had an uneasy perception that I was already too late, if the Dinner Service had passed so soon into such hands.

Turvey badly needed a shave. I tramped in the wake of his enthusiasm past more showcases of Wessex prehistory into a committee room, where a long table narrowed into the distance. It was heaped with slithering mounds of paper.

'The whole thing's here, the sum of the parts,' Turvey said. His hands produced further chaos as he tried by shuffling papers to emphasise the scope and complexity of the treasure that lay at his fingertips.

Evidence of hasty refreshment marked Turvey's trail of research throughout the night. A small triangle of French cheese stood on the drawing of a dish, at once recognisable as a sketch for the Dinner Service. It was of Lewes.

Some half-eaten chocolate was bunched in silver foil on a flattened pagoda of manuscript written in a spidery hand, which I judged to be that of Cyril Fentiman.

Perched on a corner of the table, an empty litre of Spanish burgundy had made several ruby rings across the polished surface. It damply stamped a ground-plan of the massive pantries of Potsdam, *circa* 1914, when the Kaiser had taken delivery of the Dinner Service.

The whole mess troubled me.

'This is the heart of it,' Turvey said, extending his hand over the papers in nervous blessing. 'I had to stay here all night, the car's broken down, and we live out there somewhere' – he waved northwards – 'in a caravan. An arresting life-style, you know. I've learnt, as you have, that as we get older, and Nietzsche says more mature, we have to stay mobile. Though it's a pity about the car, I was hoping to use it to dash over to Germany.'

'You mean, that's where the Dinner Service is?'

'Dinner Service?'

Desmond paused blankly, then looked at me with abstruse cunning. 'Of course, I knew you'd know about the Dinner Service,' he said generously. Then with mock severity he looked down his nose. 'Doubtless, like our friend Ranston, you think it the only masterpiece of the twentieth century. Each to his taste.'

He appeared to reconsider this put-down. Was he perhaps devaluing the papers and thereby his status? 'Anyway I've got it all here.' His fingers caressed a heap of stationery, of which a few sheets slid to the floor. I glimpsed a sketch of a Norman keep floating, the downs behind it zigzagging in air. 'Well, not here exactly. It depends on your definition of place. But the secrets are all in these documents, if only we can get it together.'

'May I read them, Desmond?'

'That's another matter.'

'They can't be confidential after so long.'

'I sort of have them in trust. For the nation, so to speak.'

'Not even a glance?'

'You wouldn't know what you were up against,' Desmond said with a petulant flick of the hand, almost toppling the empty bottle off the table.

This wobble sprang an idea, one that usually works on reluctant informers. I said, 'For old times' sake . . .'

'I did say no, comrade.'

'Wait – for old times' sake, Desmond, let's have a bite on me at that wine-bar you mentioned. Unless you're too busy?'

'Well . . .' he cocked his head and gave another mad sidelong grin, as boyish as ever. 'Still friends?'

'Naturally.'

Reversing the usual process, Turvey's method of refreshing his system was to chew wine solidly down his throat in mouthfuls, while sipping judiciously at fragments of food. I felt aggrieved not to be sharing the drink with him, but I decided for once on lunchtime sobriety, if only to conserve funds. There were other reasons.

So I let a frosty glass of Muscadet go warm while he, reaching out to the bottle through swathes of the deviously metaphysical, polished off the rest. A flask of not inconsiderable Chianti (I tasted it) vanished towards his vocal cords in exchange for ever more meandering talk about the difficulties of reconciling marriage and art, or girls and marriage, or art and life, or marriage and anything. Which equations he meted out in spasms of self-discovery.

He then, at my insistence, still failing to note how abstemious I was, irrigated his verbiage with not one but two large glasses of vintage port. These he masticated in long convulsions of the jaw, washing them down with an occasional driblet of Stilton.

Meanwhile he enlarged on his circumstances and asked me nothing of mine. He managed to give me the impression that I was still awaiting the results of my degree, while he had surged forward and taken life by the throat.

Turvey then paused, surrounded by empty glasses, and gazed bravely at me through the half-closed eyes of a man who thought he was thinking.

'Where's that bloody waitress?' he said.

'I've paid. It's closed. We have the place to ourselves.' I paused. 'Shall we wander back?'

He slowly winced. 'I often take a nap in the afternoons,' he said. 'I'm my own master, my own man. The boss. I do my own will and wish. I have this tiny room in some student's flat – get it? You've got it. Where's that girl?'

He swung round, angling his chair with a squeak on two unsteady feet. 'I brook no delays.'

'Who'll be looking after the shop for you?'

'Shop?' Turvey said. His eyes bright with wit, he sought an epigram. 'I have nothing to sell but my sex.'

'So I can keep an eye on the papers while you're otherwise engaged?'

A moment's doubt hung dangerously in his eye. Then: 'It will be all right with everyone concerned,' he said airily. 'You have my authority, that's good enough for me.' His hands scuffled with the paid bill, made play with a pen. On the back of my bill he illegibly wrote, 'Pass the bearer without let or hindrance', in a line that slid off the edge, muttered with accuracy, 'You swine,' and signed it.

Turvey then sidled with soft knees towards the unisex door to the lavatories, missed it by inches, hands flailing out to bodega walls for support, and somehow shouldered his way into the waitress who had served us.

'Are you of no fixed address?' he said seductively, voice gobbling.

She was pretty and she grinned and put out a hand to steady him. I thought with acid humour of that rocking punt all those years ago. And left them to it.

Nobody at the museum stopped me as I waved the signed bill. Simple explanation: there was nobody on guard. I could have swiped all the arrowheads I wanted.

The past was mine for the taking.

I looked at the long room and breathed in, then sat down.

Fentiman's papers, though in chaos, testified to the discipline of an orderly man. During hours of search – no Turvey, no one else – I came to know and enjoy him as an idealised reflection of myself.

The old boy was born in 1885. He reached conclusions about the twentieth century's death-wish almost before it had dawned. In the early 1900s he held the teenage view that his beloved England was racing downhill into self-inflicted wars.

Amazing stuff for a schoolboy. He almost seemed to be

personally initiating the decline of the west before anyone else had thought of such a silly idea.

All this was expressed over the years in the modest prose of journals that were intended to clarify his own spirit, not to convert. He thought it already too late to tell anyone to stop it.

At the same time his affection for the savour of life – watching the weather, growing things, collecting – was that of an enthusiast trying to diminish the dictatorial potency of time and raise his vision to novel levels of understanding.

All very poignant. He knew that civilisation had only just begun, yet was about to be destroyed.

1914 found him surprised by his sudden patriotism. But also hounded by guilt. The guilt was harder to bear. Shouldn't he have uttered a warning? Might he not by personal intervention have checked the race to war?

This did seem a mad exaggeration of his abilities, megalomania gone crazy. But his very intensity persuaded me that he had possessed the power to reverse history, if he had known how to exploit it.

A bit of his lunacy had obviously rubbed off on me. Yet I found in him an inspiration that somewhere accorded with buried feelings of my own.

His was a voice that gently urged me on.

Despite every encouragement to dismiss him as the kind of eccentric who pesters newspapers with quires of utopian balderdash, these writings of his had a seam of hope, the existence of which had never occurred to me, or anyone I knew, since we grew up. That each of us, by himself, unaided, could achieve something of moment.

That was the message.

I sat eating the rest of Turvey's chocolate and I thought about this absurd view with an excitement that made it difficult to think.

Then after 1914 Fentiman's diary went mute. His few judgments were reserved. He noted only his enthusiams.

He added to his collections – of early glassware, Tudor books, biblical statuary, pebbles, shells – in a bid to complete them. Or at least to cushion his life in the timeless. Or to exist in a vacuum of his own making.

Yet haunting undertows of pain ruminated beneath the few notes he left annually. He appeared to be avoiding contentment on purpose, in case he liked it.

When Hitler was making the news, Fentiman set off on a solitary walk to Berlin, to see for himself. And there he observed a small glass case of pottery in the Stadtsmuseum.

Three or four exquisite pieces, one chipped, another cracked in half and repaired with lead struts, bore images of an England which, before the war, he had felt would soon vanish for good.

Chatsworth was the cracked one. The twin spires of the cathedral at Lichfield had a chip missing. A dingle near Ripon, with a sweep of dales mystifying the distance, was complete, but for a scraped glaze.

Fentiman noticed that all this fine work had been done at Stoke-on-Trent, in the heart of England, before 1914. He was much moved by it – as I was on seeing the church in which I was married – without knowing why. He came out into the streets of Berlin to catch his train home, full of an optimism which, while making no sense, ridiculed every strutting uniform he saw, every band brassily humiliating his emotions, and all politics.

This was the best moment. I finished Turvey's chocolate. On his return home Fentiman made, of course, just the enquiries I was pursuing now.

First Fentiman ran to earth a veritable colossus of the potbanks. The man who between 1911 and 1914 had been responsible at Wedgwoods for coordinating art and science in the manufacture of the Dinner Service. The great Henry Smurthwaite.

By then he was well over eighty. Retired to a detached house rattled by the trams grinding up the Waterloo Road towards Burslem, Smurthwaite remembered little but the sorrows he had undergone since history carried his life's work to Germany. And thence oblivion.

War in 1914 had simply conjured the Dinner Service out of existence.

From accompanying its delivery to Berlin by boat and train, Smurthwaite knew that his entire range of landscapes, fixed seemingly for ever, had been used once, perhaps once only, for a state banquet at Potsdam in the late July of that casually horrific summer.

He had been present in the kitchens, eyes skinned for breakages, so tensed by first-night nerves that he almost dropped one of his own soup-ladles. It had had the market-hall of Abingdon on it. Where was it now?

The dinner proceeded with due magnificence. Generals eager for battle had mopped up their gravy on the Weald of Kent or Leeds Town Hall, while the cutlery of their ladies tinkled on bell-towers, ruins, dreaming spires. Diplomats seeking last-minute alternatives to war had poured cream on to their trifles from jugs bearing the very country-houses to which they would soon be retiring in comfortable ignominy.

And the Kaiser himself, inspecting a haunch of boar obscuring with its juices the frontage of Buckingham Palace, had consumed, with that summary vision of all England dominating the tables around him, one of his last peaceful meals.

The ironies of all this were embedded for ever in Smurthwaite's memory. Those ironies slowly poisoned him, as one after another his three sons fell, Ypres, Gallipoli, the Somme. And all died.

Smurthwaite had never forgiven the Germans for rewarding his years of service to their art with the murder of his sons. To locate these boys again he had immured his mind in the limiting comforts of spiritualism, while striving to forget the loss of his finest work.

On his behalf Wedgwoods had made enquiries of successive German governments after the war, each short-lived. No minister bothered to answer letters addressed to his predecessor in failure. In his grief Smurthwaite knew only that his Dinner Service had been, if not totally destroyed, dispersed – scattered pieces of a puzzle with which he identified so closely that never since had he found any order or point in life.

A pathos in Smurthwaite's confusion, as he sat in solitude trying to force his retreating brain to distinguish between his lost sons and the work of art that was also buried somewhere in Europe, touched Fentiman hard, gripped his imagination.

I felt it too, I felt my feelings soften.

The old potter, gross and grumpy, immovable in a deep chair drinking tumblers of sherry, was bothered that people, people now, people in the future, would never locate the graves of his boys.

Were they overgrown? Were the tracks to those terrains from the north of Belgium to the edge of Turkey no longer signposted?

Smurthwaite had gone just once to London. To stand breathing noisily before the tomb of the Unknown Soldier – he who might be any son of his, picked up stripped of flesh and identity, brought home to be honoured in Westminster Abbey, an edifice with which in painstaking detail he decorated one of the larger dishes, now no doubt broken or lost too, of the Dinner Service.

Were there no signs left of anything? Nothing left from before the war?

Listening to this senile muddle of the two things that had snapped Smurthwaite's life in half, Fentiman realised that his pity had been stunningly displaced by elation.

Here was a positive outcome for his long years of guilt, indecision, apathy. Indeed, patriotism. He emerged into the

Waterloo Road, trams jangling their noisy flashes of illumination past his ears in the rain, determined at all costs to search for the Dinner Service, which other people had stupidly lost.

A gravy-boat, even at this last minute, could be a grail. Each plate a patten of sacred memory.

So – 1939. Half a year before Europe tumbled again into war. And the man was fantastic – his diaries amazed me by the amount he had accomplished in so threatened a time. The very map was shifting under Fentiman's feet as Hitler began chewing up the carpet of Europe.

In his jottings I found an itinerary that covered the continent. First he sailed north-east to Sweden. Then a long sweep south brought him through Austria to the Balkans and Crete. Back to a fortnight of Rome. Up again by changes of overnight train to Copenhagen, then by the low countries south-west to Paris, down to Marseilles; and at last, via Geneva, back to England in the nick of time.

Fentiman had assembled no physical evidence of the treasure. He was content with good notions of where much of the Dinner Service was now lodged, into whose hands bits had fallen and why they hung on to them – always noting the places where pieces had found their way after the German Empire was dismantled in 1919.

I took down a lot of addresses.

But Fentiman, covering all this ground in a few weeks, had somehow turned the Dinner Service into a product of his mind. In these notes he captured his feeling that, if he held the whole pattern of the masterpiece unshakeably in his thoughts, the Dinner Service would survive for him, scattered though it was, with just as valid a reality as if he had literally gathered it all from the ends of the earth into his Hampshire cottage.

Too sanguine for me, this argument. But he meant it.

One event was typical of many, if grander than most.

In March 1939, between cities, he paused in Holland to meet

the Kaiser, still living in exile where the royal train had borne him in 1918.

No problem gaining admission to Doorn, the neat bleak castle tucked into woods where the Kaiser sawed logs or sat at his desk on a cavalry saddle. Fentiman had simply presented a letter from the editor of the *Hampshire Chronicle*, a fellow Quaker, asking how the Kaiser would preserve peace if recalled to the German throne.

The Kaiser, flatly ignored by the Führer, had learnt the value of whatever publicity he could muster. Fentiman had been urged smartly into the imperial presence by curt guards and treated to an hour of self-vindication so craven that he was almost glad the old beaver could remember nothing of any Dinner Service he had ordered in his days of majesty. His memory hadn't so much failed as become regally selective.

At this point, beaming with a thin aristocratic senility, the Kaiser rose to terminate the audience, and as Fentiman turned a slant of late sun struck across some glass-fronted shelves, and there they were. The Severn Estuary caught luminously in a prismatic glaze. Angles of light cutting into an image of Edinburgh haloed by storm-clouds.

The Kaiser stood, hunched, smile on the fade, awaiting the end of an event that had already passed from his mind. A waxwork guard stood inside the door, a glove on the handle.

Fentiman was aware of being in limbo a second too soon. He could hardly move for the brilliance of what he had just seen, the questions it posed. Yet the moment for a postscript had passed. He had to go. Already the Kaiser's back was turning, the last of the sun drew off the shelves, twilight invaded the elaborate furniture.

Bowing out, Fentiman plodded after a guard into a hall where a footman was lighting the lamps. He had briefly seen all he wanted.

He had merely not asked about it. Or obtained it for himself. And that was where he and I parted company.

I wanted it all.

It was very late when I found I could absorb no more. Well after eleven. Nobody knew where I was. Turvey had typically forgotten me. It was no surprise to find that I was now locked into the museum. Like an exhibit.

Putting the papers into final order, or rather a disorder which Turvey would recognise as his own, I came across the sketch of Lewes which he had let slip.

It was an image of some delicacy, done in ink and wash, with care. The old High Street lifted a double stave of rooflines in a curved crescendo towards the Castle, behind which the Downs were rinsed in water-colour as blue as a dream.

Timelessly decorative. But a sudden hatred of the place, of all such places, overcame me – for existing then with such apparent permanence, for deteriorating into the fumes and modish rusticity of now. Ringed by petrol stations – I knew Lewes well – occupied by urban countrymen commuting to the cheats of big business, the town had become, like much of England, a showpiece not worth a glance. I had an urge to destroy Lewes.

Or steal it, why not? It belonged only to the past. I put the drawing in a folder, on which Turvey had scribbled some ridiculous mnemonic, and slipped it under my jacket.

In the basement, where the boilers looked even more extinct than the arrowheads, I found a window that could be forced. As narrow as a frame for the sketch of Lewes, giving on to an alley. Through a cobwebbed pane the tower of the cathedral was still floodlit with arty restraint, as if washed by a luminous yesterday. Not a soul was in sight.

Using a poker to ease up the flap, I clambered over a heap of coal and slithered into real air that smelt of country.

The High Street looked empty, a print of itself. Lamps cast

unmoving shadows of medieval outlines. A vague rumpus, as from a tavern, billowed out of the silence, faded, then returned as clipped footsteps.

And suddenly men, two or three, swivelled out of a byway, and without pause an arm swung, a body lunging with a grunt across the pavement, and I was down. And my strength ebbed. I couldn't understand, stone grazing my cheek, how I had no strength.

The three men breathed round my head in a flurry of movement, hands dug into my inside pocket, a shoulder lifted me half into the gutter as I swiped out at a dark close eye that jerked back, and Lewes slithered along the flags where someone jumped on it, hissed, picked it up, slapped my wallet against it – and they were away, all in ten seconds.

I knelt to my feet, anaesthetised by pain. Only later I felt the throb in my head, a juddered arm. Now just the humiliation and loss registered. A town I had won by stealth had been casually stolen back from me by an exercise of brutality.

When they found out what the sketch was, how useless to them, they would drop it in pieces down a drain. And with a sneer strip the wallet of its money, worth nothing in comparison.

Touching the sore cheek, infuriated by loss, I found the car standing alone, with a ticket, in a square of tarmac overhung by that smug mellow cut-out of the cathedral. Unlike most victims, I could quite believe the violence; as commonplace as a belch. Yet I felt a different rage – being immorally cheated of an object which I had surrendered my moral equilibrium to obtain. How about that?

In this fit of pique I abandoned the car and strode off looking for a hotel. It was chillingly late to find a hot bath. Among my pet hates – such as muggers, museums, men I knew at college, thieves, sweetbreads and wives, to name only a handful – the provincial hotel stands high. Such was my rage that I wanted almost to court disappointment.

And I was suitably disappointed. The Wessex had a room, dammit, a bath, a sandwich, a drink, another drink, and from my window a view of the cathedral that looked as ancient and touching as an item from the Dinner Service.

Nothing seemed very real, except me and my cheque-book.

Over breakfast, if only to be sure of the reality of the Dinner Service, I decided to move on to Bournemouth.

I wanted to know where Myra Tremlett had found West Dole. If my church still existed – the one where I got married – more of the Dinner Service might be somewhere under my nose.

Between the amiable swells of the Hampshire downs I drove west along roads that soon tunnelled into the old spaces of the New Forest – itself doubtless depicted on a plate long vanished into some ruined part of Europe. I kept wondering how the heroic Fentiman would have dealt with last night's violent reversal in the fortunes of the Dinner Service.

Philosophic, glad, furious? All three, and more. I began to think that no reaction – to anything – was half enough.

In the arcade where Mrs Tremlett had her shop an organ was pumping out old favourites to a dozy audience of wheelchairs. She was alone, as usual. With the flattering poise of a woman waiting exclusively for me.

I inspected her stock, half hoping to find among the wobbling pagodas of china on dresser shelves some piece of the Dinner Service. But also – I'd fancied her on the drive – wondering what to say.

Memory had played me the usual trick of supposing her attractive. Of course she was far too fat. All right, today she looked fairly slim in a sort of loose dress. But I knew that when she moved she would waddle at once from the ease of youth into a middle age of some amplitude.

And she would smell of powder, of flesh relaxed by the passage of time.

Meanwhile, with the sentimental organ wheezing an even older favourite down the arcade, she stood at a statuesque remove, waiting for me to put a foot wrong.

'One of your influential friends,' she said at length, 'has been on the telephone to me.'

'Now who would that be? I don't recollect any.' Then: 'The fact is I'm looking for more pieces similar to the sauce-tureen, Myra.'

'Courtney Ranston. Quite an honour,' Mrs Tremlett said. 'He's after the same things, it would seem.'

'That doesn't surprise me.'

'No?'

'He knows my wife.'

'I know.' She gazed up at me, her pupils small and steady. 'Good. I was wondering how he knows you have that little church. Being close to the government, I suppose – they know more about us than we do ourselves, don't they?'

I drew slightly away from her. No hardship. But at the scent of betrayal more anger than ever stirred in me, a really knotty anger. Outside a loud pedal was sustaining a very long note. Her eyes sought to ogle me in an attempt at conspiracy.

'Perhaps,' she said, 'you have friends in the media who might have told Courtney Ranston about us' – she paused a second – 'me selling it, I mean, and you buying it. It was such a beautiful thing, wasn't it?'

'Come off it, Myra. You know perfectly well my wife works for a newspaper.'

'Oh, but I'm quite at a loss,' Mrs Tremlett said. 'Do tell me why everyone is so interested.'

I drew a breath. The bitch. She swayed, biting the upper edge of her full lower lip. The organ launched another selection, pounding the arcade with too much deafening sound like blood drumming in the ears.

Time to be honest. But also hard. I said, 'It's important to me, this. A tiny part of a much bigger thing, you know.' Her eyes flickered. 'I may be mad, but I can't bear to leave it alone. You understand?'

'I do,' she said.

'Then help me.'

'I will,' she said hoarsely, a catch in the throat.

I smelt her breath. Not good. A bit of hair touched my chin, wirily, exuding a sour scent. The music poured over our heads, rumbling a deep note through the guts of the furniture.

'Oh,' said Mrs Tremlett regretfully.

She reached up, with a sort of misery, and pecked my lips. A silly thrill passed into me. Women! Somewhere I had lost the thread.

'Very nice,' I murmured.

I had mislaid vocabulary too. Once over, this desiccated kiss wasn't nice at all. Even less nice because I felt an urge to discover if it would be nicer the second time. Whereas it was a deflection. Vaguely it made me stop wanting to know about the Dinner Service.

A final chord rattled the glass in the roof of the arcade and applause echoed from the wheelchairs.

'Let's have lunch together, Roland,' she said gently. 'Then I'll willingly take you to the people who sold me the tureen.'

We lunched at the Royal Bath, overlooking the shimmer of the sea towards Studland.

She ate her way through a dozen oysters, a woodcock and a sherry trifle. Peculiarly riveting was her manner of sloppily vacuuming oysters into her mouth, then dabbing juice off her chin as that mouth formed words. She seemed to be defining sensuality.

And when her mouth wasn't full her heart was. Either she was gazing at me with a solemnity easily mistaken for pity, or she was suggesting what a beautiful view the shimmer of the sea towards Studland must offer from the bedrooms. Or her hand was poised spiderishly on the table within reach of mine. Or she was sadly listening to me deflecting her questions about my wife. A considerable heat was refracted off the sea through the plate-glass windows.

Staring at this plumply dainty raptor perched on her chair, I began to feel guilty. Guilty that I had failed to take the hand or book the bedroom, even guiltier because more than once, as her lips endlessly chewed and sucked the game, I wanted to do both.

Then over the coffee she said, 'Do you really need to go and meet my contact?', and I gazed at her mouth for a second, then nodded. She also nodded, if more slowly, then pursed her lips.

Taking my arm comfortably as we passed reception, she murmured, 'We have all the time in the world, Mr Patcham.' In a voice lush with threat.

Basil Duckworth lived on the fringes of Wareham in an ancestral monstrosity thinly veiled by saplings.

I got ready to do some hearty disliking as Myra Tremlett whispered the scenario close to my ear. In a surround of rumpled fields that sagged towards the horizon stood an outcrop of cheap bungalows designed by Duckworth, but developed on land presented to Mrs Duckworth by her rich father.

At his last gasp this old man, detesting Duckworth's greedy ruination of an unspoilt corner of England, had sold off his belongings to local dealers for next to nothing, so that his son-in-law wouldn't inherit the small fortune they might have realised. It would have gone on drink.

Mrs Tremlett had taken advantage of all this, of course. She had paid only a few pence for West Dole in a job-lot of precious china. She also knew that the dying man, for reasons of family association, had withheld one piece of the Dinner Service – Lindisfarne, she thought – as a last sentimental gift to his daughter who had so painfully erred in marrying Duckworth.

My task was to charm her into parting with it or at least giving me a look.

The door was snatched open by a gaunt unsteady figure with a depressed moustache, whose manners had long since dissolved in whisky.

'Yes?' he said, greeting Mrs Tremlett with a stare of outrage.

Could we see his wife?

'Certainly not,' he said, reacting as to an obscene suggestion. 'I know you, don't think I don't. We've nothing to say to people of your stamp.'

Behind him lay an unfurnished hall with a scrap of worn rug in the middle.

'Forgive this intrusion,' I said tightly, 'but your name was given me by the Director of National Arts as a man who . . .'

'Arts,' said Duckworth. 'Arts. What's that to do with me? I don't pay taxes to have people telling me what I'm supposed to like. Anyway I've had your kind here before.'

This muddled bluster smacked of guilt. Alcohol was advertising the secret that Duckworth had something to hide.

'Paying public money through the nose,' he went on, 'to cheat us out of what's rightfully ours, that's what it is. Bad enough having a daughter who costs a fortune getting no bloody where in the ballet. Why don't you subsidise her?'

Behind this display of logic some garish clothes materialised and a loose-sleeved hand caught his elbow. 'What is it, dear, can I help, what are these nice visitors wanting?'

Mrs Duckworth's figure filled to capacity some long and flowing and patterned silks, doubtless an ethnic gift from her dancing daughter. 'Do come in, all of you,' she said, and without grace Duckworth loped off, his steps clacking unevenly on bare boards.

We entered a panelled room of some age and merit where voids gaped between one or two antiques in hopeless need of repair. Chairbacks creaked. Seats seesawed.

'Basil has left us to attend to the administration of the estate,'

Mrs Duckworth said as if repeating a falsehood by rote. She planted an inch or so of uncertain smile on the middle distance.

'It's about that very nice dish your father left you,' Mrs Tremlett said. 'My friend would love to see it.'

'And so he shall – I prize it so, it's quite the most beautiful thing. Basil always says you could have your dinner off it, and of course people did – that is, before it came to be thought of as art.' She vaguely snapped her fingers, as if summoning a servant or a memory. 'Now where did I put it?'

She floated from the room. I had an intuition that no good would come of this visit. In the silence the emptiness of the present cast a long shadow across spaces designed for luxury. The pathos of it echoed over the huge gap between Mrs Tremlett's faulty chair and mine. Again I could feel her eyes trying to engage me. Her mouth was moving slightly as though swallowing oysters. I longed to leave. Time had been wasted here for so long that it seemed to have gone somewhere else.

Upstairs there was a rapid scutter on bare boards, an exchange of words that buffeted back and forth in a void just out of hearing, a boom of someone hurrying under the vault of the hall, and then Mrs Duckworth returned with tears in her eyes.

Her face had a cramped look, all features closed. She turned to Mrs Tremlett. Evidently no mere man could measure the weight of her loss.

'Basil is too busy at his papers to come and tell you himself,' she said. 'It's very hard for him to keep going in present circumstances, you see, but he has had to cut his losses and find a buyer for father's gift to me, and of course to prevent my being hurt he couldn't possibly have told me about it.'

She looked for the first time at me. 'Isn't it dreadful to be disappointed over a thing you felt so strongly about?'

The burden of emotion put the question beyond an answer. One could only be practical.

'Who bought it, Mrs Duckworth?' I said.

'Oh, you kind man, you can't get it back for me,' she said. 'A gentleman called Mr Ranston telephoned only yesterday and sent someone to fetch it. He said he was buying it for the nation.'

'How much did the nation pay?'

'Oh, something nominal, they said. Twenty pounds, was it? But Basil considered it his public duty. And we're getting our name in the catalogue.'

I smiled wanly at her, suppressing rage.

'Yes, I suppose that's a comfort,' she said.

The early London air tasted of metal. Yet far away of spring too. It was 8 a.m. and I drove through thin traffic to Sophie's newspaper at the rear of Fleet Street.

I had given the worst years of my life to that same paper. I remembered the place; the place had forgotten me.

A glum janitor, despite notices about security, slouched in his chair and nodded. I took the lift to the top floor, where a number of chars were lobbing gossip over the whine of hoovers in open-plan offices.

I found Sophie's desk.

And I almost didn't notice my old familiar, the smell of newsprint on the inky air. I sat down and breathed it in. It caught me unawares. I had missed it.

Feeling moved, and pretty rotten, and hurt, I blinked at Sophie's desk.

The surface was clear except for a paper-clip and a diary blank for that day. I flipped through it. Every day was blank.

Either her secrets were elsewhere or she didn't exist.

Then I started on the drawers. The file was fattish and marked IGDS, as by 'we cognos'. Leaning it against her typewriter I began leafing through the evidence of the conspiracy against me.

My paranoia vanished. I really was being edged out.

The first letter in after the Dinner Service mention in her column was a sloshed scrawl from Basil Duckworth. He was preposterously demanding two hundred quid for Lindisfarne. That was a week old.

The most recent item was a flimsy of a letter to Courtney Ranston. Signed by Sophie, phrased with an oily collusion that had their special relationship wriggling between the lines, the letter thanked the Director of National Arts for that splendid breakfast at the Savoy and, as promised, enclosed stats of several later communications from readers who claimed to possess parts of the Dinner Service.

Ranston might wish to follow these up, it went on. Meanwhile how exciting that HRH had expressed such a personal interest in their little search!

The originals of the letters were in the file, attached by staple to the copy of Sophie's syrupy note.

I hated her.

The addresses of these people – a 'cross-section', as Sophie wittily put it – were miles apart.

Some horsey dame had gushed out a confession on sky-blue paper from a high-sounding residence in Herefs. A card, posted in Cumbria, had a squiggled signature that looked self-destructive. From Cornwall a sheet of cartridge paper had the message enclosed within the printed outline of a vase; the correspondent was a local potter.

I scanned with annoyance a typed effusion from a London dealer called Julian Budbury – hadn't I interviewed him once? – who could apparently deploy on request an encyclopaedic knowledge of the Dinner Service. A ramble in broken English came from a German living at a Leicester address.

Enough. I skipped the rest. Sophie had buried the real loonies at the bottom of the file.

But it was evident that each of these varying responses to her request for information was genuine. And also felt, warmly felt. They weren't in it for a bottle of hock. Or a mention. Or money.

They had written in with excitement, recognising something

very real of their own in the vague description they had read in the paper.

And they were waiting.

It was now Monday. The package had been sent to Ranston by last Friday's post. Unless so dedicated to art that he worked weekends, unlikely for a chap who subsidised the Savoy with taxpayer's money, Ranston would be opening these letters – I looked at my watch – within an hour. Or, given the leisurely habits of deskbound dictators of our culture, three hours.

In other words he might just have time to read his morning's mail, if not act upon it, before investing more public funds in luncheon at this club or that.

I had the whole of today. At best, if the posts played up as usual, tomorrow too. Good grief, what a caper! A vision of all England coming within my grasp briefly seized the roots of my imagination. With luck I could get those pieces before anyone else did.

I had no conscience about using my old office's facilities. If Sophie had sold out to the Establishment, so by extension had her newspaper. I recalled where the copying machine was. Next to a grubby kettle, near the tea-bags, a few yards from where the Arts staff took pride in controlling civilised values by phone.

Cleaners homed in, trying to place me. But I stuck to the job. The machine choked, jumped, chewed paper, then at length blurred its way through the whole of Sophie's secrets.

I walked downstairs with the swag. Rarely except on my wedding day – and not really then, it's just a joke – had I been faced with so much to do in such a short time with so alarming a prospect of failure.

For an hour I could ill afford I waited for Julian Budbury.

His gallery in Cork Street was a warren of art on several floors connected by narrow passages. Result: you couldn't look properly at one masterpiece without backing into another.

One or two girls masquerading as hidden cameras kept a

snooty eye on me, as I wandered up and down forming the view that all this exorbitant trash was no match for a single item in the Dinner Service. The telephones kept ringing.

Now and then a girl brought me up to date on Budbury's whereabouts.

He had left home, but called in somewhere to pick up something.

He couldn't find any taxis.

Then he had to stop at some hotel to discuss some point with someone.

I knew nothing about Budbury except his name, his taste in underpaid slavery and his neurotic timetable. But from afar he exerted on me an irresistible pressure not to like him. Even his absence unnerved me.

At last he arrived, a busy figure bursting out of a tight twill suit. Who reeled off puffy instructions to the girls as if to revitalise them. Who pretended not to notice his visitor.

I gathered the instant mistrust was mutual. Especially as he now swung round, hand out, with a glimmering affability, narrowing his eyes. Our hands touched with a damp shock.

'Ah, you've been reading our Sophie,' he said. 'Well, the short answer is – yes and no. Reporters are paid to make mistakes so that experts can correct them, but of course we know that Courtney Ranston is behind it, don't we? A nice man, a good man in his way, a friend, but do you really go for those narrowed eyes?'

'I'm afraid I rather like him.'

'Don't be afraid. Fear is what he trades on, he consumes other people's nerves for supper, you know the type. Hence the low profile – I'm not yet ready to talk turkey about this Dinner Service he's trying to give us all angst about. I'll sell, yes – but I'll wait. I'll wait until someone thinks they need me to complete the set. That's business, if not art. It'll never happen, of course.'

'You can't assume that.'

'Can't I?' Budbury said. 'I had a friend in the sixties who thought, as some of us did then, that he could find the secret of life by chasing it all over the continent. Maurice Bone – always travelling light, which usually means making heavy weather of things, no? But he did carry around with him just this one quite coruscating image.'

'What of?'

'King's College Cambridge, would you believe it? My college. He'd never been near the place. So why? You tell me. He was mad, of course. That's one piece you'll never find, Patcham, though I'd give a lot for it.'

'What happened to him?'

'Bone? Oh, a fearful idealist. He died in Iceland on a glacier, I heard, probably still thinking he could melt it single-handed. My poor old college must have gone down a crevasse.'

'But I'm told you have some pieces yourself.'

'I own Rugby – just the school,' Budbury said. 'I think a mile or two of the Devon coast is mine. Yes, and there's Brighton, rather a muddle, with a not very good glimpse of the Lanes – that belongs to me. One other – where is it? Oh yes, the Menai Straits, but who cares about Wales?'

Not all these places meant much to me. But the fact of their existence close at hand made me want them – to recognise them as part of my private heritage – and to increase their stature by adding to them whatever else I would find later. Oh God, how wrong, so wrong, that Budbury shouldn't care what the pictures represented or judge them of individual value as parts of a unique whole.

So they were to be hidden. Kept apart until someone, following a fashion, paid him more than someone else, who had set that fashion.

He was juggling with the bloody plates.

'Might I look at them?'

'No point, Patcham, no point. The asking price, which I'm at liberty to change if you show any sign of agreeing to it, is one thousand pounds sterling per piece. And I'd need a clearance from Ranston. How can I be sure as a responsible dealer that you're collecting for love? Not everyone might approve of our great country falling into private hands, you realise. You might want to take it abroad or give it to your kids for Christmas or feed it into a washing-up machine. How am I to know?'

'That's a ridiculous price.'

'Ah, Patcham, it might be worth it.'

In the background a pretty slave mimed a question at Budbury. With a thin smile he snatched up a telephone, spoke a few words, then covered the mouthpiece with a plump hand, again narrowing his eyes.

'Come back when the cashflow improves and I'll show you the pieces,' he said. 'Don't forget the magic maxim, old boy – we're all in business.'

At the bank I withdrew five hundred pounds, almost the last of my leaden handshake from the paper.

At the travel agency I wrote a cheque for a first-class single to Paris the day after tomorrow. One had to start somewhere.

At my club – the only institution, including marriage, that hadn't booted me out – I sat in a hot cubicle with the L-R directory on my knee.

In 1939 Anton Moritz was a dealer in Hamburg. When Fentiman dropped into his premises, he had been so preoccupied with imminent departure that he was convinced Fentiman had come to arrest him.

Having booked passage to England that night under an assumed name, Moritz was in a dither over what to take into exile. His waistcoat pockets bulged with gold rings. Fentiman claimed to have seen in the shop several pieces of the Dinner Service (including a luminous view of Malmesbury backed by a rainbow) which, by persuading Moritz of their potential value in the London sale-rooms, he had induced him to add to his luggage – if only as an act of homage to the country of his intended refuge. They had agreed to meet in London.

What had happened to this man, then in his thirties, who must have been one of the last Jews to slip the net?

I patiently began by phoning Alexander. The search ended ten minutes later and halfway through the alphabet with Maria.

Yes, she had a brother called Anton.

No, he was no longer in England.

Yes, she was elderly, her heating had broken down, her room was in Kensal Green, she had bad neighbours, she couldn't live on her pension.

No, she hadn't seen her brother for years, but he sent her presents from Antwerp.

Yes, they were gifts of money, and she would be dead without them.

Yes, she was lucky to be alive. Some weren't.

My hand holding the phone was clammy with tension. Anton's address? A pause, a snort, a hiss of papers being sifted, a few sighs. I hardly dared ask his profession for fear of being wrong.

Yes, he had a shop.

No – with a despairing hack of a laugh – it wasn't silver or gold these days.

'He is selling weapons,' she said.

I rang off shaking. I had my first foothold in Europe.

At noon, at last, I set off westward. I reckoned that snapping up 5 pieces of the Dinner Service from Sophie's fan-mail would put me in the running – at least show the Arts boys I meant business.

But really I had no thoughts. I just drove. I suppose I'd hoped to view and feel something of an England which I'd ignored for years. Time was against sightseeing, however. Tame landscapes switchbacked at speed around me. Straight roads turned nasty at blind bends. The car hastened up bald hills to divulge countrysides forming out of mist. An estuary ebbed away. It all looked like memory. I was in too great a hurry to merit much reality.

That went for the people too. Met, greeted, talked to, left, they all faded back into the drone of the engine. First, a cottage daintily camouflaged by trees near Stroud, a barrel-chested giant, Major Trumper, retired from the Control Commission after years in Germany: high spirits, honesty, a huge man fiddling with exact hobbies like carpentry, linocuts, scale models. Big dogs just out of quarantine paced the small garden. An unseen wife was dismembering Bach with a violin in an upstairs room. 'Good to meet a chap with the guts to take on a challenge,' Trumper said. He sold me his dinner-plate of Durham, acquired in the aftermath of war from a fat fräulein who had flattered his homesickness by serving him eggs and bacon on it. A fellow called Humphrey Booth, bored stiff in our consulate at Hamburg, would also be glad to help if he could. Total cost: 50 quid, 45 minutes.

To the tip of Cornwall, where the potter lived. Over the blowy heights of Dartmoor, then lanes narrowing towards the Atlantic, gulls swerving over the car in panic. Between rhododendrons a drive retreated from the present into a nineteenth century where gales rattled the windows: an old rectory converted into studios. Bill Tracy was hosting the fag-end of a bottle party in a peeling parlour shelved like a showroom with crudely thrown pots and jugs, and we ended up after midnight sitting cross-legged on cushions, eating mince and peas off paper plates, owls outside, looking at Salisbury Cathedral in the lap of water meadows on a serving dish. 'Christ, the delicacy of it all,' Tracy said. 'I wish I'd made it, that sort of craft's going, going, gone.' He was drunk. Would he take fifty for it? 'Turning corners, that's what art is,' he said drowsily. 'For my own work to be any good I need to suffer the loss. Say a hundred.' He needed the money. I spent a short night on a hard floor, departing at dawn, no breakfast.

The outskirts of Hereford by lunchtime, Trumper forgotten, Tracy a shadow. Well-dressed parkland lifted in drapes from the road. Mrs Driver's cottage: a small nursery specialising in herbs. 'But the piece is an heirloom,' she murmured. The little rooms within were furnished with a medley of such heirlooms, wreathed in green plants writhing to black beams. Elderflower wine lubricated the discussion. How prettily upright she looked, dinky knees crossed, in the elaborate frame of a home that was almost asphyxiating her. An odd herbal warmth crept down my limbs, as her knees strained through green tights. Myself exercising charm at a remove, all sense of time destroyed. The Isle of Wight was up in her bedroom. On the way a landing swayed. On the wall a bearded man in a frame, her father killed at Dunkirk, cajoled me a step further. The Isle of Wight, hazy beauty, chalk cliffs in a mist, memories stirring. I kissed her. Ten minutes later she was handing me a neat parcel tied with raffia. 'I want nothing for it, it's far too precious,' she said. Cost: one hour and ten minutes, a kiss, a digestion contorted by nerves, a promise to return and dine and talk and stay when my collection was complete.

Leicester under wet lamplight hours later, crescents trailing off in curves of parked cars to vistas of bungalows as flat as caravans. Kurt Muller, German, ex-prisoner-of-war, in service to a Mr Pinner, away on holiday in Belgium. In every room store cupboards fronted by asbestos doors, protecting pillars of tinned foods, a one-man supermarket: Mr Pinner's provisions in case of nuclear war included a year's supply of toilet rolls. Muller displaying this terrific foresight with a naïve pride in his employer's superiority, while refusing to talk of the Dinner Service. He knew too much, wanted nothing more to do with it, was frightened. Then Muller came clean. That afternoon a visit from a National Arts district organiser, one Chalmers, enquiring after the two items in his possession, namely the Severn Estuary and Edinburgh. Instant recall: Fentiman had seen these at Doorn, they had belonged to the Kaiser. Where had

Muller found them? It took an hour to winkle out his story of service to the imperial household as a lad, between 1938 and 1941 when the Kaiser died, and his theft. Where were the pieces now? In Mr Pinner's safe, to which he alone had the key, sandwiched between the stacks of bottled fruit and enough fishpaste for an army. Muller was afraid, not only of nuclear war, but of his residence permit being withdrawn if he didn't hand the pieces over to Chalmers, who had pulled rank. Would money help? Yes, one hundred pounds for an option on the pieces, sight unseen, in exchange for a written promise that Muller would hold them until I returned from abroad. We shook on it, he with a wet palm. Present tally: over 500 miles, more than 20 gallons of petrol, 1 headache, no food, 3 items of the Dinner Service wrapped up in the boot, 2 gone into hiding, a kiss and a promise, all at a cost that I no longer dared add up.

An hotel? You must be joking. I settled for a long doze in a car-park after eggs, sausages, bacon, chips and beans: two more pounds. I would miss the booked train to Paris. I needed two pieces more. Finance got on my nerves. People just met faded from my mind. Nuclear war threatened. Time was getting even shorter. But then I awoke and the motorway drew me north through unfocused country in the dark, names of towns blinking off boards as if they no longer existed, Manchester aching under clouds to the west, Liverpool a dim glow. Dawn over the Lake District looked washed-out and alien. I did some more dozing in a lay-by overlooking Ullswater, awaiting a civilised hour to confront my last chance.

I pulled a long chain in a lofty porch, the bell reverberating in faraway kitchens. A wait. There was a crippled boathouse. The lake was ringed by banks of evergreen that glittered dull silver in the rain. I was too tired to know where I was, except at the right address.

Hilary Smith was an ageing elongated widow, walking angularly, with a grim smile, living alone in this ramble of a house, someone's Gothic dream released into folly. A game of chess was poised at a difficult check, patience laid out, a half-finished patchwork quilt spread over a sofa like a dust-sheet. Abandoned by her family – one son an explorer, two at universities abroad – she occupied this crumbling home with only ancestors, pictured on the walls, to keep it from moral decay; physically it had started to disintegrate when the industrial revolution's cash ran out. The house was ice-cold. Her brother William had elected to live in the South of France, and there on holiday, in the cellars of a grand castle he was renovating, she had found a dessert plate, but in pieces, which pictured this very house: a jigsaw bundled into a sack with lots of other broken china left behind. Drinking coffee I tried to put the jumble of pieces in order, while she read her letters, just delivered: one from Ranston, others with foreign stamps. I knew from the look of things – turrets glittering, high summer, Ullswater in a glaze of romance – that at short notice she wouldn't sell me that shattered plate. But could I not borrow it, repair it, enjoy it for a while, bring it back to her? 'I don't think you're a rogue,' she said, preparing a receipt, which I signed. She sealed her fragments of the Dinner Service into a manila envelope. Expenditure: two hours of persuasion, no cash, a promise.

Hilary Smith was my last call based on the letters stolen from Sophie.

I was a day late. But I had beaten my official rivals by gathering up in the nick of time a few unique pieces of the Dinner Service, three perfect, one flawed, two in safe keeping.

Very good.

The length of England drizzled past the hard shoulder and driving home to London took me five hours of noisy anonymity. Dimly I kept seeing signposts to soup-ladles. Views I might shortly own emerged from the mists. For once I felt I was getting it together.

But despite my ticket to the continent I had a compulsion to go home, see my cargo unpacked, set it up in my own space. Childish? Maybe. And show it all to Sophie.

I now very much wanted Sophie to share in the Dinner Service – for itself, yes, for the beauty of what I had so far accumulated, for whatever it was going to mean, for my initiative in getting off my behind, for doing my damnedest to thwart the vain ambitions of her even vainer lover. But also as an act of hate. I mean love.

'I have it on good authority,' Sophie said, 'that you've been making a thorough nuisance of yourself.'

As a surprise for my wife we were breakfasting off the Dinner Service. I had put the cream for her coffee into the sauce-tureen of the church at West Dole. Overnight I had mended Ullswater so that she could use it for her toast. For the second time in its history Durham was serving bacon and eggs, and I had the Isle of Wight in front of me, smeared with marmalade.

These histrionics had cut no ice.

Not that I'd meant to be theatrical. I was intrigued by the idea that objects so long out of circulation were once again being put to practical use – lying between us on the stripped pine not as a gesture, as nothing so sentimental as a peace-offering. But as the first glimpse of a terra nova of my own, which I simply wanted to share with someone else.

Sophie's view was nervously different.

Indeed she pretended to ignore the china, while also avoiding my eye. This meant continuously looking out of the window, where squalls of rain were trying to mask the council flats.

'I'm not used,' she said, 'to having my breakfast on stolen property.'

'You're not used to having breakfast with me.'

'Who are you, Roland? I don't seem to know any more. You're always running off to rifle people's private files or cheat them out of their belongings.' She poured a dribble of cream out of the nuptial church. 'Are you a terrorist or something? Why can't you leave these affairs to people who know about them? I only ask for your sake.'

'Do you really not know what I'm doing, Sophie?'

'I've heard enough of the truth to know that your version will be entirely different,' she said with indifference.

A spasm of sexual fury caught me in the stomach, too like desire to be comfortable. My brilliant scheme for breakfast now seemed grotesque; the Dinner Service had no reality at all, except in my mind. Its bits and pieces stood on the table with the pathos of a mistimed grandeur which only I understood.

'I know I've said this before . . .'

'Say it again, darling,' she murmured in ominous invitation. 'Do feel free to say it all again.'

'You don't make it easy . . .'

'It's never easy.'

'But I do think for once, Sophie, that I've found the key. The whole answer.'

'Forgive me,' she said. 'To what, exactly?'

'All right, to lack of purpose, lack of faith, the ghastly neurotic thing of aching for something more in life – well, just my old problem of having bugger-all to do that I think's worth doing.'

'That's not a problem. It's you. It's why we love you. Why didn't you take up a sort of hobby instead? I'd have supported you. Something like – well, pottery. You might have made some money at it.'

'Listen, Sophie – those plates haven't got any value you can assess, we're not talking about money.'

'Oh, he's so obvious,' she murmured in brackets.

'They're only a tiny part of the Imperial German Dinner Service.'

'Don't do this to me,' she muttered.

'The whole caboodle runs to over a thousand pieces, it's the most wonderful picture of England ever made if you look at it closely enough.'

'I've heard it all before,' she groaned.

'And it still exists, it's all over the place, Sophie, in collections, people hoarding it under beds, people not knowing its worth, and nobody any longer looking at it as a whole or caring what has happened to it, so this intensely English thing of beauty, which everyone's going to think a joy for ever as soon as I get hold of it, is scattered all over the continent, and look, it's already aroused more passion in me, just listen, Sophie, don't stare out of the bloody window, than anything since I fell in love with you. So I'm buggered if I'm not going off to find it.'

She picked up West Dole. Helped herself to the last of the cream. Rain pattered on the glass. She looked spoilt.

'It's just a metaphor, isn't it?'

'Metaphor? Where the hell did you dig up that word?'

'I mean, you're looking for the hidden significance, right?'

'My brain doesn't know what metaphors are, Sophie. They send it to sleep. Nothing is enough like anything else to be worth the figure of speech it's printed on. I want the thing itself. But complete.'

'The way you wanted me?'

'With the same passion.'

Sophie smirked. 'I don't want to inconvenience your passion, sweetie,' she said levelly, 'but when are you thinking of leaving your wife?'

'I'm not leaving you.'

'You've wanted to for ages.'

'Rubbish.'

'You can't take it, can you?'

'Most of it.'

'You just can't cope with being dependent on me, letting me be free. You're not man enough.'

'Balls.'

'You haven't enough feeling in you to accept the responsibility for a one-to-one relationship, it's too great a strain on your vanity, you're too small.'

There was no point in disputing any of these threadbare offcuts of the couch. She had given the matter no thought – or too much feeling. Her emotions obviously felt like brains.

In any case she seemed to be quoting, the phrases weren't hers, any more than her mention of metaphor was, so they didn't cut deep, not at all, so I waited.

Her fingers went out and just touched the lip of a plate. Silence. Fingertips not quite reaching the cocked head of the eagle.

'Oh, dear . . .'

The voice faltered slightly.

I still didn't budge or utter a word.

Then she said, 'It's too bad', hunched, dropped her forehead with a soft knock on the table, not quite assaulting a piece of the Dinner Service, saying 'Oh, dear' again, flailing her hair to and fro in a hubbub of mute tears. Her back heaved.

I saw the catch of her bra straining through wool.

The Isle of Wight glittered in a brief flush of sunlight from the window.

Painfully I said nothing.

'It's so silly, but when are you going?' Sophie said.

'Today.'

Sophie said, 'Today.' Then stood, severely handsome, still acting a part, quoting someone else at each turn of the argument, and moved to the door.

'Forgive me – I must use the phone,' she said. 'It's only fair. I must claim the right to stop you making a big mistake, and I must help you, darling, that's what I'm here for.'

She left. I picked up my knife. I sat amid the detritus of a noble breakfast destroyed in mood by the petty conduct of a woman I loved. Without appetite, scraping butter off a transept of Salisbury Cathedral, I ate a piece of toast, hearing the modulations of her voice on the phone in hushed echo from the hall.

I then cleaned the crumbs and egg off the Dinner Service and packed it in tissue paper. Her voice in the hall whispered on, now and then rising to a muffled cry.

I knew better than to eavesdrop; there was nothing in anyone else's life that I wanted to hear. Instead I filled a grip with shirts and socks, while trying to savour an anticipation of the continent that awaited me and my discoveries. This became hard when Sophie started heaving sobs into the receiver. It sounded as though the house had asthma.

She must have been on the line to Ranston for half an hour. Then she stood, a waif, at the bedroom door, with a look of downright innocence.

'Your best man would like a few words with you,' she said.

'I've nothing to say to my worst enemy.'

'Darling, I beseech you to do one small thing for me.'

'I'm the tiniest bit busy . . .'

'Because I love you,' Sophie said.

True – or not true? I strutted to the phone in a pet, determined to deflect whatever manipulation was planned for me.

'Yes?'

'Old friend?' The gravelly, humouring tones sounded as young as ever. 'Our little bird tells me you're off abroad today.'

'Yes?'

'Lucky fellow. It so happens I've cancelled a speaking engagement for this evening.'

'Really?'

'So if you were generously to postpone your trip we could get together.'

'Why?'

The tone changed not very subtly, no less genial but without irony. 'Because I can help you. You must know that. We have interests in common.' The irony slipped back, making me feel somehow detestable. 'Used we not to confer?'

'What have you in mind?'

'A quiet dinner at – my club, let's say.'

'And the agenda, Courtney?'

'If you're still a claret man I'll see to it you're not disappointed,' he said.

'No – no, come clean.' I felt confused, with no excuse for confusion. 'What's it all about?'

'You know better than to ask an operator like me a question like that.' I could hear him smiling, enjoying the risks he was taking with my temper. 'Besides, you might come prepared. Let's keep our surprises up our sleeves, shall we? Do indulge me, Roland. Eightish?'

'Mr Ranston is expecting me.'

'He's not here as yet, sir. Perhaps you'd care to wait in his private room.'

This sounded unsatisfactory. It presaged a session of political psychiatry with me cast as the patient.

Or were there to be other guests?

I threaded my way between the bald heads armchaired in a snoozing mockery of death. The carpeted silences breathed asphyxiation. I poured myself sherry in a room panelled with flickering books, where the table piled with flowers looked like a lying-in-state, if not a metaphor.

Yes, four places were laid. I was trying to guess who would turn up when they all did. A timed entry: Courtney Ranston flanked by a pair of departmental colleagues. I was told their names but missed them.

Ranston had kept his looks so well preserved that he had begun to resemble his caricatures. The lean nose, the sensually laconic twist of the mouth. The honest stare that merely suggested blindness. Brackets of iron-grey hair.

Sophie's lover. Once my best friend.

He grasped my hand, then withdrew into his elegance. And sherry.

A few compliments were exchanged on the nature of art. I listened with some care, but instantly forgot what anyone said.

Then a club servant, with ceremony, brought in an oval

platter covered to its edges with thinly sliced smoked salmon. 'Ah,' said Ranston significantly or perhaps just with appetite. For a few seconds art receded as a topic, until we had helped ourselves.

This revealed the plate's perimeter, which had vine-leaves all round it. By now the others were affecting not to look at me, while digging in. More of the picture underneath the smoked salmon came smudgily into view.

I had an impression of gothic pinnacles on a skyline.

Ranston then inched forward with his fork, as if inviting photography, and took the last slice. This unveiled the Palace of Westminster.

Was I supposed to be impressed?

Mind you, the candles did solemnify the Abbey. Over the scene the light bulged, then receded, fluttering as though to set the picture in motion. Lots of little Londoners were performing their forgotten antics around the square. It all looked nervously alive, or less dead than when I walked through the reality. Under a patina of grease from the salmon the tall church glinted pink as from a sunset, moving me with the calm of her eight centuries at the heart of things.

It was obscene that these men were eating off it for mere effect. More than ever I felt committed to lone search.

'It's the centre-piece,' murmured Ranston. 'The heart of the thing.' It sounded false.

Out of this spurious hush of admiration for the piece Ranston now looked at me as though wanting to be looked at. The loose smile offered me his own assessment of his powers, indeed his power. His thin, red, slightly devilish face was both imposing and ridiculous. It was assuming its superiority. The whole thing was as posed or poised as a photograph.

'Old chum,' he said with a flash of intimacy, 'we're relying on you, you know.'

'I haven't the least idea what you mean.'

'Not to stand in the way.'

'Of what?'

'We are collecting,' he said weightily, as if nobody had thought of it before, 'the Imperial German Dinner Service.'

'So am I.'

'His Royal Highness is behind us. He's taking a very personal interest.'

'So I hear.'

'Yes, but I must place before you certain facts.'

'I'm not interested, Courtney. My position's very simple . . .'

'Or beliefs, rather than facts. I believe most firmly in this country and her welfare, as do you, and in her future, as we must, and indeed in her past. I also believe in private enterprise, but of course for the public good.'

'Yes, I suppose that's why you're having an affair with my wife,' I said equably. 'Are these gentlemen aware of that footnote to the conspiracy?'

Give him his due. Without a tremor he went on, 'Do put me right, Roland. I can't imagine you want to own this masterpiece yourself. To buy it up wherever you find it or can afford it – and you'll run into difficulties there – and then hide it away in the exclusive privacy of your own collection, when you could be sharing it with the nation.'

'Look, Courtney, this was Sophie's idea first off. Is that why you want it?'

'I want this for England,' Ranston snapped, then relaxed. 'Nobody's said anything as unfashionable as that for half a century, but I'm prepared to go down as a sentimentalist – having come up as a cynic, eh?'

'I wouldn't put it that way,' said one of the men, smiling.

'We're in the realm of ideals,' said the other, grinning.

'Just think, Roland,' Ranston said. 'Think if anyone else snatches the Dinner Service off us – there are rumours – before we get off our backsides and go out there and fight for it. Or keeps it to himself when really, you know, it does belong to this country. We started it. We made it. Just consider that – something so essentially ours, expressing all our genius, coming home at last.'

I said nothing.

The plain fact was that I couldn't make up my mind. Despite feeling diminished by Ranston's rhetorical pranks, by appearances that were not just deceptive but false, by a certainty that Sophie had let me in for these blandishments, I had to admit that not only did Courtney's words, though hollow, convey much of my own respect and liking for the Dinner Service, but also that getting out tempted me.

Let others do it.

Yet some lack of spirit in these men, their taste for easy options, their readiness to compromise, kept holding me back.

I couldn't say yes or no, which wasn't fighting fair, but felt right.

I began, 'Just a second . . .'

But Ranston raised a hand, then in ceremony his glass, which now contained the promised claret.

'To the Imperial German Dinner Service,' he said with sepulchral finesse, as if burying it. 'Why, you ask, is it so immensely important? Because I know that the British people – perhaps ever since 1914, when they stopped knowing where they stood – want me, want us, and that happily includes the royal family, to find some means of showing them, reminding them, what kind of people they really are. Courageous, inventive, original, yes, and backed by the best of all possible pasts – but that tradition must, of course, inspire us to an even greater future.'

Nothing wrong with these words. They just had too much of the right ring.

'So – the Dinner Service!' Ranston said. 'Keep out of it, old friend. Help us by forgetting it. We need it here. We are going to get back from our old enemies what properly belongs to us.'

It still sounded false, if true. Anyway it was all too much.

'For pity's sake let's leave it at that,' I said.

Ranston said evenly, 'If you so wish.'

For the remainder of the meal – roast pork, several vegetables, flans with sundry fruits in them, various cheeses, lots of undoubtedly good claret – we discussed in general evasions the rights and wrongs of looking for the Dinner Service as a matter of principle: thin high-table stuff, the English mind at its effusive nadir, drowning thought and feeling in irony and wine.

Ranston, for example, seemed with a devilish advocacy to be against the operation, but spoke cunningly in its favour, then allowed himself to be convinced, albeit with reservations. The others, busy inserting the plums into their own next harvest of prose, listened with punctilio to every word without hearing any. I, though drawn generously into the vacuum of these deliberations, said little.

There was little to say which I could mean.

In the end nothing had changed except the number of brain-cells destroyed by the workings of alcohol and vanity, and I had spent much of the dinner gazing at the flickering plate – the club servants having been forbidden to remove the heart of democracy – as if that alone were still the key to my escape.

Or confrontation.

The charmed circle broke up on the stroke of midnight.

'Good man,' Ranston said, entering a limousine.

I slept on it.

I had a hamper made up at my club. And cashed a cheque with the secretary for £400, trusting my balance would cover it. And lodged my small share of the Dinner Service in his safe. And took a taxi to Victoria.

The warmth of a first-class corner! The spring winds ripped across the undulations of Kent with the shivery illusion that England was being torn out of my grasp. I was to travel from Dover the old way. An expeditionary force arriving just in time, the start of the grand tour, a crusade.

A sense of physical well-being, unknown to me since youth, accompanied this act of getting out.

The icy winds across the quay at Dover put me into a turmoil. I almost believed that no moment more real had ever impinged on my life.

I was prepared for the boat being a disappointment. Most of the lounge seats were occupied by knapsacks and plastic carriers. Their owners were massed round the duty-free store or lining up in a cafeteria that reeked of chips. Drifts of youth in jeans moved with hostile agility through groups of elderly package couples. Gone the grandeur of anticipation, gone the savour of approaching abroad. Class had now bowed out.

Never mind, I had brought my own style with me.

The ship shuddered once. Finding a space I got to grips with the hamper. Somewhere a glass shattered.

After wiping milky tea-stains off the table top I covered it with a linen napkin. Laid it with the club's cutlery and glass. And put out a dinner plate.

We had reached the open sea. Soon such a plate, recovered by me from neglect, would bear an image of the White Cliffs. I looked back appropriately at the original swaying through the window. Then set to. England was soon blotted out by a thick vinaigrette that went with the artichoke.

Voices quietened as the sea roughened.

One or two alien beards stared briefly my way, cans of beer in hand. My helping of smoked eel – lemon, nip of horseradish – enlarged the silence round me. The ship lolled in the waves, then soared.

People were moving away. Out of dry ice I drew half a bottle of Pouilly Fuissé which I drank slowly – thinking back to Romney Marsh, oasthouses near Tenterden with orchards lapping them, the pebble beaches west of Folkestone. All of which had suspended their meaning until I found them again somewhere hidden in the mists of Europe ahead.

The bar emptied towards the lavatories. The boat kicked.

And here I was, at last, approaching Europe in high fettle, serving myself cold breast of partridge, potato salad, a bottle of Volnay, in full health and appetite, with a fine intention of solving all our problems at a stroke and leading a new life into the inexhaustible future.

I could have hugged myself.

Beyond the window young men staggered off to the scuppers. The labelled old were sicking up where the flags roared against the wind. Meanwhile I tackled the Stilton, heard the ping of a buoy, and saw the forlorn coastline of Belgium passing, with not a metaphor in sight.

I gazed out. And thanked God that somehow one thing in life always meant another. And that nothing for a moment was only itself. And that I had discovered this in middle age with enough time left to prove it.

Or was this too metaphorical? And was I pissed?

And why did Sophie's remark nag me?

And why hadn't I told Ranston honestly that he could go to hell?

When I reached the first-class bit of the train to Antwerp a restaurant car was looking for business. Half a dozen smart chaps were juggling to and fro a lunch that put to shame the vulgar snobbery of my refreshment on the boat.

Served me right.

I fell heavily asleep until a suburb of Brussels glided past like the beginnings of a headache. Was it myself that I wasn't being honest with?

I stepped off at Antwerp. The high vault reverberated with renewed confidence. I had cabled Anton Moritz, saying that I would call and why.

In the Groenplads I checked into a toppling hotel supported by buildings of equally medieval decrepitude. Then found the alley, dominated by the hulk of the cathedral, where Moritz had his workshop.

It was a moment of some feeling.

* * *

A glass case of old weaponry served as a counter. Beyond a Gothic wooden partition that gave his tiny premises the mood of a chantry, Moritz was peaceably burnishing the blade of a sword under a bulb. On the dark walls bayonets flashed above jumbled stacks of pottery.

I tapped a finger on the glass. Moritz started out of his privacy. A small neat man in his seventies, a dome fringed by absent-minded hair, a sharp beard jutting off his chin.

'Mr Patcham?' he asked with husky courtesy, sword in hand.

'None other.'

'You have perhaps a passport?'

'A passport?'

'I am in the habit of making sure.'

'Of what?'

He eyed my photograph as if valuing a miniature. Then said, 'Didn't I spend five years as a guest of the Germans? I prefer not to do business with them.' With the sword he made a jerky pass at his shadow. 'How did you find me?'

I told him. Fentiman's note: Moritz had escaped from Hamburg in '39, taking to the safety of England certain Dinner Service items.

'Oh, no, if only I had,' Moritz said. 'I made the mistake of bringing some goods to a friend, one honourable German among the few or so I thought, to look after for me in Hamburg, including these beautiful dishes that interest you. He would keep them faithfully until Hitler was finished with. Wolfgang Rolle, a good antiquarian, a friend, and he promised me, he did promise. I do not know if he made a telephone call to anyone, but at the boat, just as your English seamen were loosening the ropes, I was arrested. You know what happened. Everyone knows what happened.'

As we all do, I involuntarily glanced at his arm for the faded tattoo of a number. He was wearing a pullover to the ball of his thumb.

'Yes,' he said.

A silence ensued. Uneasily solemn.

Moritz's eyes were almost too gentle with trust. He seemed to be placing me under an obligation even more binding than my duty to myself.

I felt guiltily out of this league – this pain dissolved by humour, but somehow seeking a relentless publicity – this hatred now borne with more relish than suffering, but spilling over to anyone who had missed feeling it.

To my annoyance I said, 'I'm sorry.'

This produced a dry cackle.

'I did not mean to embarrass you, except that you asked me,' he said. 'It happened that when your doctors at Belsen had kindly put my body to rights, I did return to Hamburg, which was of course in the ruins that your bombing planes had made, and I saw with tears, with tears indeed, that my friend Wolfgang Rolle's street was mostly flat, and they had been great houses suitable for rich men. They all died, you know, but I hadn't.'

Moritz put down the sword.

Far from sounding like senile reminiscence, his story was evidently far more alive to him than the present moment. Yet it had an over-rehearsed air, as if no repetition could get it finally off his chest. His eyes were greedily fixed on me.

'I waited until the night,' he said. 'Then like the rats picked my way through the pile of brick, which had once been good civilised rooms, and found below the stairs the door to the cellar where all my treasure would be.' He smiled faintly. 'No one should be so anxious to possess,' he said. 'I felt so certain of finding all Rolle had hidden from his stock against the air-raids that it tasted as juicy in the mouth as a revenge. Like killing him again for what he had done to me.'

Moritz shrugged. 'There was nothing, of course. It had been looted. I stood there striking matches – it was so damp they fizzled out. The only things left were the stove, the pots and pans which the family had used when they came down to shelter from your airplanes. And then with almost the last match I looked at the plates they had been using to feed them during those terrible nights. Still smeared with food.' He paused with a chuckle. 'You know what these plates were?'

'I do.'

'They were not broken or scratched or hurt.'

'Even total war can't destroy everything.'

'Nor did I break them, as I took them away, five of them, one for each of that German family, who died in an English raid.'

There was nothing to say. My diaphragm felt strained. I was aware of the bare bulb paining me.

Tears had sprung easily into his eyes. The shadows of the workshop no longer seemed quite real, but laced with layer upon layer of association glinting from the old-fashioned weapons – history stretching confusedly back to include every murder, every act of betrayal. And every miraculous twist of fortune.

Again Moritz shrugged with mild humour, as if indeed personifying the ironies of history. And that too looked vulgarly rehearsed. I was much moved by the recovery of the plates. But half felt, again guiltily, that I had been deceived into someone else's emotions – and my own would come later, if at all.

Yes, if at all. Where were my feelings? I was beginning to think I had never plumbed them.

'So you still have the pieces?'

He opened his hands to me. 'For the past months I have not kept them here. Whoever wants them in Germany will do much to obtain them, I think.'

'Does somebody in Germany want them?'

'I will tell you. But if you would like to see them?'

'Very much.'

'Follow me. I am for my sins an assistant to the Hofmeister.'

The workshop's back door led us under an eroded arch to a side entry into the cathedral, which Moritz opened with an oiled key. It was musky inside. Shadows thickened away from one sharp point of light suspended in the chancel.

My unease in his company deepened. The density of alien religion dogged me up a spiral staircase, footsteps clanging in the vault with an echo of hostility. I had an apprehension of literally rising into the unknown.

In the organ loft Moritz unlocked a cupboard let into the panelled case. It was heaped with sheet music. Jagged brown corners of notation littered the floor amid mouse droppings. Moritz moved aside about fifteen hours of the likes of Buxtehude to uncover a small crate that had once contained Sicilian lemons – and drew out the plates wrapped in old copies of *Le Monde*.

Every time a plate emerged he placed it on the organ stool. Then turned aside to fold the newspaper in neat squares.

At first I saw on the china only dim shapes of the possibly familiar. Then Moritz flicked on the striplight above the console, revealing the keys and stops of the organ's massed resources. And at once I was in the presence of places I knew.

The unfamiliarity receded. The Black Mountains loomed out of the smell of incense. I glimpsed busy courts in the City of London compressed into the centre of a serving platter, I saw the sands and seas of the Suffolk coast widen to a thin line of habitation on the horizon, possibly Aldeburgh. And there, a reminder of home blessings in this void of a cathedral, stood in miniature the church of St Mary Redcliffe, evoking the poet Chatterton and his young death, the sherry trade, the lure of the maritime sketched into the gulls that sculled over Bristol.

Moritz stood behind me, still folding, his fingers nervous. Mice had eaten cut-outs in *Le Monde*.

As I took them in briefly I put the plates back one on top of another, with some naïve sense of preserving a charm that might fade. Or possibly saving up the real enjoyment for later, as a child might. And at that moment Moritz swung his legs on to the stool, touching the button that operated the wind supply.

A giant sigh, rather like deafness, breathed out into the body of the church, followed by the stridency, unravelling in slow rhythms as intimately regular as the sight of one's own heart on a cardiograph, of the opening line of a fugue I knew.

I put a possessive hand on the pile of plates and listened.

The counterpoint grew more complicated, but I could still follow it, if only in memory. One voice after another entered, in different tones, a breathy flute outlining the hidden contours of those Welsh mountains, a diapason reverberating through that crowded glimpse of a London which the Germans had tried to flatten and cow, an endless wash of sea and land and sky in the sway of the harmonies.

All parts of me. Long lost. Or long ignored.

My mind thought it knew, without bothering to explain, that these moments poised here in Antwerp on the edge of Europe were touching upon – not art or memory – neither sentiment nor association – but on some undertow to reality as yet unnoticed by me, some principle of life as yet untackled. How to put it? A truth to which I might be too dim ever to have access, but which was there for the taking. And this pained me with an uprush of pleasure, of understanding, which it held just out of reach.

I liked the feeling. It tempted me on. It was something of my own. It was whole.

The music drew to a long halt in the major. I weighed the plates in my hand, wondering how to bargain for them.

Moritz took them and wrapped them up again. We came out together into the cold air. Mingled aromas from the restaurants gave the evening its first tasty edge. I was hungry again.

The little man seemed smaller standing in his workshop. Back came the solemn unease of his race or of mine. We were still deeply in accord, but only just. He waited for me to speak, perhaps to make an offer, but I was refusing him that pleasure, so he said casually, 'I am giving you these plates, not because I wish to, but on conditions.'

I said, 'Of course I was going to pay you for them.'

'You will pay my sister in London what the pieces are worth to you.'

At once I saw the nature of obligation as he viewed it: he had to be totally in the right or, if not, I must be totally in his debt. Here was history manipulating the present.

'And you will also promise never to sell these pieces,' he went on. 'They belong to all of us, you see. Not just you English.'

'I think I know that,' I said, knowing nothing for sure.

'That is art,' he murmured, tapping the newspaper. 'It is also history. It is civilisation . . . Are you sure all this is not too much for you?'

'I expect I'll recover.'

Moritz looked at me for some time. His door was open on the alley. People passed as quickly as shadows. I smelt mussels cooking in an odorous sauce. Fried potatoes, wafts of coffee. Was he waiting for me to find a formula to thank him for his kindness? He had simply done too much for me.

Yet his sly ease was irritating. Above our heads a lavatory flushed, probably in my own hotel, a woman's cry was stopped short behind an upper window. And I blamed Moritz for those effects too – as irrelevantly emotive.

'Are we in business?' I said.

He went on looking at me. More emotions. A tram grinding round the square. Seagulls waving suddenly in the fogged light of streetlamps. On the Scheldt a ship's siren began a long fugue, then cut off.

Moritz said firmly, still as if questioning my honesty, 'You will go to Germany?'

'Of course I'm going to Germany. Don't you realise how keen I am to assemble the whole of this Dinner Service?'

It sounded snappish. His shoulders heaved.

'Yes, I do, oh, yes, I do.' A litany, but very sad, mixed with threat, still uncertain. It was as though I had agreed not only to paying his sister a fortune, but also to avenging his wrongs in the country which had both given him birth and tortured him almost to death.

What the hell was I taking on? I wanted abruptly to run away from it all.

'Then go to Germany,' he said. 'Without delay, if that is possible. If you believe really in what you are doing, you will go. You will report to me the value you place on these objects when you pay my sister, and you will tell me what you have achieved. It is of interest to us all.'

And at that moment, having struggled against the feeling, I knew. Quite simply I was prejudiced against this fellow.

I couldn't bear his instructions disguised as fondness. They were dictatorial. Great vengeful passion was stowed away behind them. His generosity triggered off in me a wariness as honest as the thoroughly civilised way he was behaving. I felt drowned in another man's inverted guilt.

Not knowing him – having no clue to his motives – I detested my own reactions to the extent of wanting to do violence to his knowingness. He flourished a wisdom that cried out to be taken down a peg or two. Perhaps I couldn't either take or match his degree of self-awareness.

Or would I have to pay more later, whatever the price I was now paying? I just felt the debt would go on and on.

Moritz spread his arms, as if inviting me to hit him. 'Now we exchange information,' he said. Over a headline stripped from *Le Monde* I wrote down my details. It felt like making over my private life to him. Yet I had every reason to like this man, even love him.

Moritz wrote a name and address on a business card, then added another. 'It is something to be Jewish, ah?' he said.

'I know,' I said.

I knew nothing. Least of all about myself.

I had gained more than I dared hope. But my pretences felt false and my aims cheap.

I possessed the objects on trust – yet had no means of paying his sister a fair price without selling them, which I was forbidden to do. Nor could I imagine selling them. Moritz had left me with the burden of believing that they belonged to me only on behalf of humanity.

I wasn't humanity by a long chalk. I was a spoilt, angry, bewildered and obsessed reporter.

I laid the pieces out on my bed. They were ravishing. They were also a definition of responsibility. I'd never had a challenge like that before. Even marriage wasn't.

For the first time I wondered if Fentiman hadn't perhaps been right in contenting himself with just glimpses of the Dinner Service.

To recover from the hangover of being emotionally manhandled by Moritz, I used the dual therapy of food and drink. Across the square, in a crypt busy with fat burghers and wives laughing their hats off over heaps of food, I worked my way through a huge creamy dish of mussels and a tall carafe of wine – hanging on to the thread of refreshment as the only way back to life through the moral labyrinth.

It worked. It usually does. Inner battles give way to ingestion.

I went to bed and fell into a grateful doze, hearing the rain, with the Black Mountains on a soup-plate held like a book in my hands.

Sophie and I years ago were splashing down long lanes between sheep. The stark line of hills undulating westward to a sunset. She had just said I could live anywhere with you and it's going on for ever my darling, and as my eyes closed over the image, rain in my ears, I had just observed that nothing in that picture – no cottage or clump of trees, hardly a ewe grazing at the roadside – had changed.

I awoke very happy in the small hours, out of a light sleep, still holding the plate, convinced that I was elsewhere.

It seemed at this moment that the Dinner Service was a

portrait of my life, certainly its past. Perhaps the future too.

There was no doubt about the present. The lace curtains were blowing inward. Above the parked trams in the square, which was wet and racing with more rain, I could see with comfort the upper windows of houses where others slept.

Nobody was about. A shiver ran down that deep valley in the mountains, and nothing was irreversible, and everything was to come. Again Sophie shouted, it's going on for ever my darling, and then I slipped away.

It was my best sleep in ages. I hadn't even broken the plate.

I got into the Hauptbahnhof in Hamburg determined, if need be, to take on the whole of Germany. Under the arch of glass waiting expresses aimed at points all over Europe, points I would take by storm. The air sharp, metallic. Everyone well dressed, busy clicking into place, running to a timetable.

I took a taxi to the Consulate and asked for Humphrey Booth. A tall disarticulated figure with a smudge of moustache – middle age was wearing him thin. But I liked his eyes. Good and poached.

'Ah,' he said, 'you're the chap looking for all this rather grand china.'

'How do you know a thing like that?'

'Note from Major Trumper to expect you.'

'Trumper?'

'Colleague of mine. Sold you a plate. Cotswolds. Got it?'

'That's fast work.'

'We're old friends. Come for lunch.'

I stepped into Booth's car, an ancient beetle.

'Anyway, nice to see you, welcome to Hamburg, etc,' he said with a thin grin, grinding gears. 'Good people, the Germans.'

'Are you sure about that?'

'Not really. But I married one, you know.'

'I look forward to meeting her.'

'You're out of luck,' Booth said. 'She's left me.'

'How rotten of her.'

'Not at all. It means I'm free to show you round the night-spots.'

'Not young women wrestling in mud?'

'Yes – ridiculous, isn't it?'

'And boys exerting themselves?'

'That sort of thing.'

'Is it so ridiculous?'

'We're rather proud of it,' Booth said.

'It will out, I suppose.'

'Better here than in some places I could mention.'

'East Grinstead?'

'I was really thinking of Tunbridge Wells, where my mother lives.'

'Wouldn't she care for it?'

'Transvestites? Good lord, no,' Booth said. 'Didn't like my wife either, mind you.'

'Because she was German?'

'Yes, and for not being too mad keen on the washing-up stakes.'

'My wife sounds not dissimilar.'

'Tell me about it,' Booth said. 'I do like a good gossip.'

We chatted our way companionably into feelings of alliance until Booth halted in a tree-fringed no man's land of compact separate houses.

'Home,' he said. 'No wife, no comforts, but plenty of booze and misery, so it's home.'

Indoors Booth's first act was to pour nicolaschkas, sugar on top of lemon on top of brandy. We sank them in silence, his mouth twisting briefly in shock.

'Ah,' he said, and lumbered to a draining-board smeared with tacky evenings alone. And poured another.

'Right,' he said. 'You're collecting up a great work of art.'

'Right.'

'And I happen to know some Germans are interested.'

'Who?'

'Oh, a lot of chaps,' Booth said airily. 'They look back at their country's history and see nobody more to their taste than – no, not Adolf, as you thought, nor yet Bismarck, a good guess, that – but Wilhelm II, Kaiser Bill. They're royalist, of course. Like us.'

'And they collect his Dinner Service?'

Head back, he gargled down his drink. 'They dig out souvenirs of his reign, yes. It's obvious, isn't it? The Germans lack a spiritual side.'

'Except perhaps Beethoven?'

'Yes, and some of the women. But what I mean is they have to have their nasty obsessions spelt out for them – in facts, in physical objects.'

'Symbols?'

'If you must. I hate the word.'

'I withdraw it.'

'Good for you.' Slicing more lemon, Booth lowered his voice. 'Actually they wear the old medals on top of corsets and suchlike – at parties, you know, ladies' underwear. There was a piece about it in *Stern*. Nobody took much notice. The abnormal is quite usual in Germany. Anyway the chap you want to see is Bodo Zinzendorf. Nothing symbolic about him. He's rich and he runs a club. So let's make a night of it. You free?'

'If you are.'

'A bite of dinner?'

'In good company.'

'Perhaps a string quartet or two at the Rathaus.'

'Good for our souls.'

'Then an hour or two on the beer at Zillertal.'

'To get us into the mood?'

'And then,' Booth said, 'we'll close in on the club some time in the wee hours and beard Bodo in his den. How does it sound?'

'Perfect.'

Booth downed his third drink. I followed suit. My throat seemed to roar in the back of my head – and my head swam.

'Now are you pissed enough to go out to lunch?' he said. 'The food's terrible in Germany, and I can't even boil a potato, let alone an egg . . .'

An eye ogled Humphrey Booth through a spyhole in a fortified door. This then remained shut a long time.

Cats in the street played among dustbins on lamplit cobbles potholed in places. Lids clanged and rolled away. The garbage stank.

I had just had my fill of string trios in a concert-hall out of which all breathable air had been driven by the heating. Every seizure of classical harmony had ended in the coda of a yawn.

Then, at Zillertal on the Reeperbahn, smoke clogging what remained of my lungs, a brass band in distended lederhosen had drowned Haydn for ever in bumptious noise. Meanwhile Booth grinned loudly at me out of some pained inner silence, drank several steins of beer in record time, only to flog off to the acres of lavatory with wet floors and come back reeking of sick. A sneer of muted triumph on his face.

He was bad company drunk. But even for him it had been impossible to talk above the so-called music. And here we were now on this hideous street in St Georg, waiting to be admitted to – what?

A foreign evaluation of the Dinner Service?

Or just a man called Bodo who had stashed away a lot of it?

Or some other secret beyond my guesswork?

At a signal we traipsed over a yard scattered with rubbish towards a dimly pink oblong of open door which wafted out a sexless smell of baby powder. A man in black tights stood silhouetted.

'Back entrance,' whispered Booth. 'That's Max.'

Max's chest was bare, and he had two breasts, full and proud. As though in milk.

'Ah, Maxine,' Booth said in familiar greeting.

Cosmetic eyes fluttered at me. I shook a strong hand. We entered a thin corridor of dressing-rooms, in and out of which a number of slim figures in body stockings were dithering, with garish items of military uniform in their hands.

'They're getting all primped up for the show,' Booth said.

We passed into the club itself. Several tables were occupied by citizens in suits. I had seen the likes of them hurrying about Hamburg all day. Now ties were a bit loose, tight expressions in danger of fracture. Haydn's sense and order, not to mention the Dinner Service, seemed far away.

Maxine's mammary glands swung low over our table. He put down a stiff little menu on a stand. What you could have was wild boar stew or smoked venison – both derived from animals hunted by the Kaiser, whose portrait hovered behind the unappetising print.

At the top of the card an eagle, rather like our friend on the Dinner Service, stood guard.

There was an aggressive border. In the dim light this seemed to be composed of medals, axe-heads, whips and taurine testicles. Probably, though, just some decorative fancy on the artist's part – such as olive-branches and doves, even vine-leaves. To check it by daylight, I slipped the card into my pocket.

At Booth's suggestion we ordered white wine. So were brought steins of beer. The atmosphere hinted that complaints would be out of order. The women would bridle or have hysterics.

The stage of this minute auditorium was hung with banners lavish in their illustration of birds of prey. These fowl were suspended from a ceiling ablaze with badly poised spotlights that half blinded me. Booth leaned close. 'It's all genuine, old boy, those bloody flags survived two wars somehow, and here they are, inspiring these awful chaps, golly, it's quite impressive, you'd never think the Huns had it in them to surprise us any more – that's unless you'd been married to one of them, of course,' he added, clearing his throat with a swill of beer. And the corner of my inner eye, without pleasure – no, with a joy that had something of hatred – saw those banners being swept into the countless battles. The battles that had slaughtered thousands while gaining no ground. The battles that had polished off an entire civilisation or two.

No wonder I had appointed myself saviour of the little that was left.

Or was I corrupt too?

Or simply drunk?

The show opened with a chorus of adolescents prancing onstage to the songs of those long roads behind the lines. Lilli Marlene was marching into Tipperary. There was no band. The gramophone was fitted with a scratchy needle. It clicked at every revolution as one or other of these lads, in obscene mockery of war, flopped down and died – only to jump up with a predatory grin and dart a handblown kiss at the audience of suits.

Upper halves were attired in field-grey uniforms. Medals clanged. Braid swung this way and that in busty arabesques. Their lower parts, clad in jackboots and just perceptible jock-straps, imitated in chorus-girl burlesque the plod into Belgium – a flickering map of which was now projected on to the white of the eagles.

I thought it all amateurish. But I felt there was passion in it.

When the gramophone ran down, their movements slowed, they dropped to their stockinged knees, faces wreathed in clownish irony. And applause broke out only when, the music expiring, they were finally on their faces breathing dust, silky behinds pushed up in an ultimate provocation.

All this was just meant to warm us up.

Maxine then came on – the star. His finely devised breasts were still bare.

Booth whispered, 'It costs a bomb, old boy, that operation.'

Lipstick in quantity encircled his pearly teeth – through which he now hissed, to the beat of a drum, a trilingual message. I couldn't understand it in German. I hesitated to believe it in French. And in English, not his best language, it was frankly incredible.

What he offered, in contorted rhythms, was a high-flown message of hope, possibly quoted from the Kaiser's many ludicrous dicta, certainly vintage 1914. Putting it mildly, his message had to do with the advantage to the world of its becoming more teutonic.

It said – that mouth agape with paint – that survival was likely for us only if we marched our way back to the ideals of the beginnings of Empire, when the individual counted so supremely that he could welcome the idea of perishing for a great cause.

It vaunted – that flawless set of teeth – the only man in modern times, the Kaiser himself, who had comprehended this essential relish to the otherwise fatiguing routine of human existence.

Long words poured through the lipstick. Inferior syntax waltzed all the sense away. Yet this speech grew louder with every beat of the drum which syncopated with the clicks on the record, until Maxine's breasts were lolloping up and down in a peroration of their own, and nobody could hear a word he said, in whatever tongue.

Then a fanfare, which got him offstage, then a blackout, in which I heard Booth's dentistry working on a fatty cube of wild boar. 'Bags of message, rather good, what?' he said in thick tones before the lights came up.

The male forms of the waitresses now bustled into the gloom around us and a cork popped. Champagne misbehaved on Booth's trousers, his chair shuddered back. 'Did we order this?' he said furiously, then giggled to excess, dabbing the neat creases with his hand. 'Oh, Bodo, so sorry, didn't see you – here's the old friend I phoned you about, Roland Patcham, the Dinner Service and all that.'

'I gather your order for wine was misunderstood, gentlemen, so please share a glass with me.'

The fizz was poured out with brio. Zinzendorf's courtly tone seemed quite out of context. I had heard such voices in libraries requesting the favour of an obscure book. The man himself was bald, with peculiarly rich eyes, eyes without vanity, and he was compact, sure of his ground, undramatic.

I raised my glass to him.

Booth swigged, then began to nod, elbow slipping off the table edge, head lolling.

For a while we just gossiped about the interesting history of the Dinner Service. Like scholars. I tried to be circumspect. He, on the other hand, had no wish to hide his knowledge – for he conveyed a neutral sense that if any battles were worth winning he had already won them.

If he were wealthy, as he was, that meant little to him too. I felt I terribly needed money, if only to match his indifference to it.

What he appeared to lack was the least thought that I had anything to offer him. Whatever he wanted he probably possessed already, though he was making no assumptions. All Zinzendorf seemed to wish, if I so chose, was to share his company with a man similarly obsessed, and he gave this compliment a lot of grace. Thus making me feel suspicious, hence ill-mannered. Yet very much at my ease.

From his amiable hints I had no doubt that he had access to far more of the Dinner Service than I could ever collect. Ten or twenty pieces, perhaps dozens – or more. But to judge in terms of quantity was vulgar.

His manner implied that, in speaking of the Dinner Service at all, he was treating me as a kindness to a view of the world which I hadn't the heart, brains, means or some other power to locate for myself. His eyes were hypnotic without bothering to try. His peace of mind was effortless.

Zinzendorf stood up. He was stocky, jowled, a bit plump. His sixties were gaining on him. By now I was looking for touches of inferiority – chinks in the armour which he hadn't troubled to put on.

'So let us meet tomorrow at my home,' he said with tranquil warmth.

'Will you be prepared to sell?'

'I am always prepared for anything.'

'Could we make it the day after?'

I needed the time. Money had to be raised. As did hope. The game had become professional.

'Yes, but please not later. I am disappearing for a while.' He smiled. 'You know, I much look forward to sharing my finds with you. Oh, how infrequently one meets a traveller on the same road!'

Zinzendorf shook hands with Booth, then waved at me friskily, then waddled off.

Booth smacked his lips. 'Bubbly,' he said. 'Good grief, isn't my little wife missing a lot? You must be sorry not to be sharing the fun with your good lady. Don't say I didn't put you in touch with the fountainhead.'

First of all there was my mother's flat to realise.

From Heathrow next morning I phoned Neville Netherby, a Mount Street estate agent, whom I had seen on and off since school – where we had been united in a healthy dislike of each other's personalities.

'It's urgent, Neville.'

'It never is,' he said.

'I'm going to make your fortune.'

'I've already made it.'

'I'll meet you anywhere, on any terms, provided it's this morning.'

He settled for my club at noon.

Apart from the last of my handshake from the paper, the only money I had was tied up in that garden flat in Clarendon Road, W11, which I had retained after mother's death as a lifeline. But never used. Too much of the past clung to it. The bleak furniture of childhood. The knobbly table-legs I banged my knees on. The out-of-reach drawers where sugary rewards were stowed.

The place was deeply dark, shadowed by a sycamore under which grew only the flowering weeds which mother picked with glee but left to die in the sink. The lease had forty years to run.

I had always kept the apartment up to the mark in case Sophie became too much for me. Or too little. I had never brought a girl here. It would have meant disarranging mother's bed.

I contemplated the Steinway, then rang round a few piano people. Her own tuners promised to be there in half an hour.

Left-wing and bourgeois, immured for years in these London shadows, mother had lived in her music. She pointed out the notes to me when I was six, as if they spoke volumes. Teachers as red as herrings were herded into my childhood to train my ear. Hopeless. I ended up at an adolescent concert stuck halfway through a sonata. Detesting music, then as now, for the amount of time and effort it took to reach no conclusion.

The picture of mother in my head: bent over Beethoven, eyes shimmering, the very notes like blots expunging from her life all the disappointments she feared. Including her son.

I would be glad to see the back of whatever she had bequeathed me.

The piano chap was dour, dressed in black. A few octaves and arpeggios drew me back to the old humiliations. Then he opened the flap and peered at the insides.

'There's a crack in the soundboard,' he said.

'Beethoven's piano had broken strings. How much?'

A plangent chord. 'People haven't the room . . .'

'Look,' I said. 'I'm not interested in bargaining. I want this monster out of the house. I know that you know that it's worth thousands. You don't even have to think of cheating me. I'm doing it myself. What's your least offer?'

'Well,' he said, 'if I can arrange to remove it this afternoon . . .' He paused. Childhood began ebbing away. 'I dare say we might go up to a couple of thousand.'

'Write the cheque.'

He wrote the cheque.

Neville Netherby was waiting dolefully at the club. Still a schoolboy, with narrow wary eyes behind thick glasses, ready to cheat if he could manage it without detection. A businessman.

Now he was perspiring over a tomato juice on a leather bench. Looking sidelong at entering members to rate their distinction. Listening with moody avarice to me. He had always had a sweaty skin.

My proposition was so simple that it almost scared me. At current prices the flat was valued at a bit over £30,000. I needed as much as I could raise. But could wait no longer than close of business today to complete. Netherby stared at a chat-show man roistering among his courtiers at the bar.

'So that's the scenario,' he said.

'You've got the money, Neville. You're quite unscrupulous enough to do an old friend down when he asks.'

'I have to see the flat.'

'Now?'

'I must think about that.'

'There isn't much time.'

'May I make a call?'

Within minutes he had summoned from the office a wiry character called MacShane, who had a long mournful head and looked blotto. He was an expert.

We took a taxi to Clarendon Road in silence. MacShane sucked his teeth on the jumpseat. He had the jaw of a bodyguard, short hair. Without interest Netherby gazed out at desirable properties. I had a stale image of him in the changing-rooms of long ago.

In the flat Netherby stood, hands in coat pockets, as if chilled, in the middle of the carpet, gazing at the walls, as if thinking. MacShane roamed at will. Significantly fingering wallpaper where it was peeling away. Turning on taps that gurgled and spat out brown liquid. Knocking cisterns with his knuckles, easing his heel on floorboards. And whistling all the time.

All this evidence was soon to be used against my price.

I had no price. Never again did I want to cast eyes on this well-dusted projection of my childhood. Let alone sleep a night in it. There were too many aspects which I liked against my will, too much detritus of memory to be painfully clung to.

But then occurred an event which I found hard to credit. Looking for an object to prod the mouldings, doubtless to bring them down in a cloud of plaster if possible, MacShane picked a stick out of the umbrella stand. It had a silver swan on the handle.

I remembered nothing of it. But when he took the bird's head in a tight grip, reared the ferrule and began shoving at the ceiling, I without warning, even to myself, fell upon the man – my body hammered into him, nudging his shoulder hard – and my hands wrested the stick from him in a farcical caricature of a duel.

'Christ!' he said viciously, cracking his skull on an object which in boyhood had composed one of the hard edges of my world.

Netherby's reaction was to raise an eyebrow. No doubt he expected such antics of a schoolfellow. The expert stood unsteadily up, rubbing his head as though to test its authenticity.

'I'm sorry,' I said. 'The thing belonged to my father, so naturally I . . .'

Yet not natural at all. I had never known my father, still less his taste in walking sticks. Why lie? Never mind, I had had enough of all this property. Property was always false. It led you to hit people with it.

'So what's your price?' I said.

'I'll think about it.'

'You haven't got long.'

'You keep saying that,' Netherby said. 'I think quickly.'

'Three this afternoon or it's off.'

'I'll think about it.'

'You keep saying that.'

'Let's call it stalemate then,' Netherby said. 'Ring me at three.'

'Are you suspicious of the deal?' I asked suspiciously.

Netherby was looking for a taxi. A hollow wind roared down Holland Park Avenue with the traffic.

'Roland,' he said. 'You offer me a snip. You're going to lose a lot of money, and I mean a lot. So can't I just wonder – you know, general interest – what you're standing to gain? Is it a girl or what? Trouble with the law? What can be so important?'

'Do you really want to know?'

'Until I find a taxi,' he said.

'Put it this way. I'm working alone against the state. On a matter I won't bore you with. I need to win. They've got it all on their side – resources, plenty of time, dozens of people, unlimited cash, public opinion, the lot. In fact they lack only one thing. They're not one man. Not mobile, fast, responsible, convinced, full of spirit, and of one mind. So I can beat them. But I do need my own money for it – nobody else's, don't offer me a loan. My own money.'

Netherby looked at me drily. 'I see, schoolboy adventure,' he said with a respect so grudging that it hovered near insult. 'I didn't know you were into idealism. At school we just thought you had a screw loose.'

'Neville, I'm only asking for money, not some notes from your analyst's doodle-pad.'

'Nor did I ask for all this guff. I just said call me at three.'

'Why not now? I want to know how much.'

'I'll think about it,' he said in despair, hailing a cab.

* * *

In the club I checked the past week's newspapers.

Apart from a brief item in *The Times* – Ranston hoping to drum up interest in a TV feature on the Dinner Service search – all I could find was a recent article by Sophie. It headed the Arts section of her paper and ran to half a page. It chilled me.

The mood was all wrong. To catch the eye a cartoonist had drawn the Kaiser hurling plates in a rage and stamping them into a map of Europe.

Worse, Sophie's coy style made the issue seem quaint and ancient.

Worse still, she was betraying me in print.

Her story was of a long-lost treasure which artists, bless them, had always known existed, but never actually seen. She quoted one or two with unfamiliar names, as if discovering them.

She then recounted her own part in the quest. With instant recognition of its worth, she had disclosed her find to people in high places – somehow royalty hovered unnamed between the lines – who had followed her lead in speculating that the Dinner Service might, if still around, prove belatedly to be an event of great cultural importance for our country.

It was the last minute, Sophie waffled, but not too late.

She had interviewed Ranston. In bed, to judge by his opacity. 'This,' he declared, 'reaffirms a tradition in craftsmanship and indeed points the way to a renaissance in our manner of appreciating forgotten areas of our past in such a way as to inspire us in the future . . .'

He had put the point better when we dined. Now 1.5 million readers were taking the true measure of the man.

Ranston also said – alas, for it sounded almost honest – 'I'm very excited about this. It's quite an operation, of course, and I'm glad to be associated with it. At this very minute we've got men in the field who believe in our project, as well they may, who see it as an adventure, which indeed it is, and who will certainly come up with the goods. We already know enough to be planning a fine exhibition which will tour the country – holding up a mirror, as it were, to the way we used to live . . .'

Sophie's last sentence, as usual, invited her readers to participate in the venture. By searching their attics for remnants of the Dinner Service – spying on other people's boxrooms – sneaking into local museums where a dish might lurk unrecognised – and in general making a nuisance of themselves to get their names in the papers.

My wife's treachery to me, perhaps to the cause, reverberated in every glossy word. The article worried me, for now in theory everyone knew. But at least I had gained the first round. I owned several pieces. There were more in the offing.

In the club I glanced at fellow-members at their lunch. Their lives were planned to the minute. They behaved as if they knew what these lives of theirs meant.

By chance mine wasn't planned. By tonight I could be anywhere. That wasn't freedom, except of movement. But at least my feet were directed towards a possible liberation from the tracks they had been plodding.

I telephoned Neville Netherby on the stroke of three.

He offered me £15,900 for my mother's flat.

Less than half its likely value.

With a further £5,000 to come if he sold it better than he hoped.

A meaningless promise.

To save me moving heavy furniture into store, he was prepared to shell out the extra £5,000 today.

And that would be the end of the deal.

Within five minutes I was at his office in Mount Street. I kept the taxi waiting.

We exchanged no words worth talking about. I signed a dictated letter. A secretary witnessed it. Netherby handed me a cheque for £20,900. My ears were burning.

The taxi got me to my bank ten minutes before closing time. How did you celebrate such a moment? I had no flowers for anyone. Hushed formalities took place behind glass. Did nobody believe the cheque?

Nor did I.

But one thing I did believe. By that sale I was at last giving my parents over to death. I knew it. There was nothing left of them now. I had to whisper it aloud to myself, but I knew it.

And it didn't matter. I was only converting my parents – all they'd accumulated, all the stuff I hadn't examined that might be worth a fortune – into the means to accomplish my ends. To assert my independence. Even achieve it. Clarendon Road, a small boy banging his knee, sweets out of reach – all that dissolved for ever in Netherby's acid cheque.

Now I had no choice. Indeed, by deliberate folly, had put myself beyond the reach of one.

Next morning at the airport in Hamburg I hired a car.

By a pleasing irony Bodo Zinzendorf lived north-east of Lübeck in Angeln – the land from which the English originally hailed. A country of meadows where cows lowed against a milky sky skimmed by seagulls.

I drove through a little town that looked stolidly Nordic. Hunched white church, besieged by narrow angled streets of white cottages. As a town not a bad bolt-hole, if needed.

A bumpy track led through the ruins of a pre-Viking village, now a jagged outline of crumbled streets, which in the dark ages had housed thousands of potential invaders. Here, outside the defensive walls, I skirted a rendezvous of jeeps, troop-carriers, tanks, preparing for an exercise. Germans *v.* British.

Zinzendorf's house was a low structure of no great age, standing alone against the iron line of the sea. Long stables formed a courtyard at the rear, white under a white sky. Scribbles of grey copse fringed the inland horizon. No other house was visible. The sea was calm and black to the east.

Zinzendorf greeted me as an old friend. We sat in deep chairs and drank schnapps.

Now and then blanks twanged in the air outside. Zinzendorf shrugged as if apologising for children at play. We discussed as negligible, if compared to amity, the political differences between our countries which had turned our century dark. Such risky but entertaining times to live in, we agreed.

We also agreed, on more schnapps, that modern society had betrayed all the old values without bothering to forge any new ones. We thought the world, as currently run, an indifferent utopia for the future of our children, if we had any.

All this talk was bland. Like passing the time of day.

Zinzendorf then told me in cruel detail of his early career as an SS officer and how this had disappointed him. No novel creed ever went far enough. You had to delve deeper into the past for a true future.

I nodded, expecting a reference to the Kaiser. There was none. A number of mortars outside spat empty noises in the woods. Zinzendorf shrugged again and poured more schnapps.

'Am I to see your pieces of the Dinner Service?'

'With great pleasure,' he said. 'I learn that a member of your royal family is interested. Are you working for him?'

'No. Only for myself.'

'For what reason?'

'I respond to it – and it excites me. So naturally I wonder why. Therefore I try to find out what it's all in aid of.'

'Surely,' Zinzendorf said, 'it's no more than a historical byway?'

'To you, perhaps. To me it's an emotional matter. I have the feeling that if I collect it all together, I shall discover myself to be a different person. Someone I never suspected was there.'

A shot thudded out, a flare signalling a new turn in the manoeuvres. Violet apocalypse against the milk-white sky.

'You realise you can never collect it all?' said Zinzendorf. 'Too many people are working against you.'

'Are you saying a man can never be completely himself, however hard he tries?'

'I'm saying that the Dinner Service will never be entirely yours. Some of it is in museums. Will you break in and steal it? And some belongs to me.'

He rose. We passed into an adjoining room jammed with furniture. We could only sidle in single file along alleys built of the past.

Nothing postdated 1920, when Zinzendorf was born. When the world he was temperamentally made for came to an end. Every surface, of marble or polished wood, was an orderly maze of objects, often ugly, now and then of a remote splendour, which expressed the taste of that world, the balance of which the Kaiser had upset for ever when he lost his war.

Lace, ceramic nosegays, postcards. Busts of royalty, medals. Engraved glass, flags, inkstands, old weapons. The very quantity was moving. This detritus of a civilisation had been abundantly gathered by a man who knew exactly what conveyed him best. And put into order, as if he were composing a physical memoir of that time. And all done with an intensity that left me in no doubt as to the chilling nature of love when so turned in upon itself.

A mirror, then. To enter by invitation a man's memory – to discover the narcissism of what mattered to him – to observe at close quarters the associations that stirred his feelings: that was the effect of this distorting, alien mirror. Zinzendorf's elegance was the product of this room.

Drugged by all this solid witness, I kept having to say inwardly: outside there is Europe, half-wrecked, drained of point, but still there, and here I am, here and now, being baited into a hush of respect, almost religious, for a set of beliefs that have gone.

I ought not to be responding. But it was no use. I was still too much like what I was seeing. I still liked it too much. Yet all it did was open up with a dreadful pathos the blank which this man now suffered at the centre of his life.

So it had been for all his sixty years. Europe had come and gone, and here were the last traces, flamboyant and complex and foolish.

'Of course it is all worth nothing,' Zinzendorf said with regret. 'Because I really do not have the intention to give it up. Or the courage.'

I now followed his glance. Through a filigreed shelf, past a bronze of Bismarck, to a back wall – and here were the plates. Thirty or more, of differing shapes – some for soup, others to crumble bread on, one sizeable dish at the summit of the display for carving a joint of meat – were arranged in overlapping order, so that each view partly obscured the one above.

They had the look of faces in a crowd. So muddled that I thought I no longer wanted or dared to look at them – for fear of a crushing disappointment or, worse, a response that was only a platitude.

I none the less skirted the obstacles in that confined space, and stared.

It was, first, an exquisite series of plates and dishes, the more finely resonant for being in concert. Indeed they were positioned, in descending rows, as strictly as a choir in performance. It would have been good to hear music. They spoke of villages tucked into hillsides. They sung of remote havens for battleships with long upright funnels, of edges of towns where gentlefolk lived, of chalklands, swamps and follies. Their half-hidden faces mapped England.

And it was then, with a flush of pleasure that reached to my fingertips, that I thought of Sophie. I must have glimpsed something up there, a corner of memory.

I stared again. Wars had changed the look of things. I couldn't be quite sure of anywhere. I had an impossible impulse to gather all those dishes into my arms – if only to take them off, and examine them at ease, and make sure they still existed.

But why Sophie? The mound of Maiden Newton in Dorset was outlined against a speckled sky where a bird hung, and in early days we had made love there once under skylarks, one spring, on springy turf.

Was that it? Did that explain the feel of her body that surged suddenly into mine? I wanted her voice on the telephone. I needed to know that she had not, like everything else, vanished.

Steadying myself on a heavy desk, I said, 'Won't you sell them?'

'You asked me that before.'

'What's the answer? Surely you don't want to keep something that morally belongs to the English?'

'Morally?' said Zinzendorf in surprise. 'What does that mean? Is it just because your people made these articles in the first place?'

'The Kaiser never paid up, you know.'

'Therefore I should give them back to you? When they have cost me money?'

'Money doesn't matter to you, does it?'

'Not a bit,' said Zinzendorf.

'Is that why you won't sell?'

'This is becoming trivial, my friend,' he said. 'I will not sell or give or even consider it, until I know how far you are ready to go for this Dinner Service – and why. By far my greatest interest at the moment lies in what you can tell me about obsession.'

I said nothing. In silence we continued our survey of England, necks cricked up. The Cotswolds in shadow were almost covered by the keep at Alfriston – when had Sophie and I last seen it? – matted in ivy, and Exmoor lay below the horizon of the dome of St Paul's. Where one midnight, it must have been Christmas – why were we in London? – we had stood holding hands, hemmed in by hundreds of others breathing carols on the cold air.

Zinzendorf went on staring, his eyes making a superior sense out of the display. But all the associations were peculiar to me. They belonged to nobody else.

It was I who had walked that autumn in Wensleydale, wondering if I wanted Sophie to close with my offer of marriage. Fearing her lethal combination of looks, ambition and temper.

I who had caught trains to my regiment from St Pancras, which loomed in a trim riot of turrets hung with smoke behind the clean lines of the Yorkshire moors.

I who had gathered the memories that one by one were fixed to that wall, almost as if I were living them again. But in a heightened life, in a time that had abandoned continuity.

The softly planted garden of a house near Buxton in a smudged dawn. The interior of a ruined abbey in the West, Tintern, caught in the monotones of dusk. The cobbles of a gabled street in Wells, where we were circuitously looking for a cream tea during a quarrel about nothing. All mine – all experiences half surrendered to oblivion – but now firmly set, in the ins and outs of shadowy lines on the plates, at a time before I was born.

By thus aligning my own recollections with a larger memory, I was within reach of making sense of both.

I looked anew at those glimpses of England. Most of them I had known, but never put together in any pattern. Closing my eyes, I now blindingly saw that my life had been worrying its way towards achieving a point – if only that of enabling me to stand here, glad and frightened, thinking these untypical thoughts. Or rather feeling them in the hollow of my chest.

'You're teaching me what obsession is,' I said. 'I never knew till now. In the normal way I'm ordinary and tired and bored and out of a job. I want to live in another spirit. And I can do that by getting it together – collecting up something that's dispersed. And never should have been dispersed. Don't forget that a golden age is depicted on those plates. So golden that people started destroying it as soon as it was born. And, dammit, I want to live in a golden age. The one that awaits me on the other side of bringing all those fragile things back home and understanding whatever they have to tell me.'

'You English – arrogant as ever,' Zinzendorf said with a smile. 'Just like your culture – unscrupulous and selfish. No wonder it's dying. Or dead.'

'I'm not dying or dead. I've proved that. By taking a hint from the Dinner Service and going beyond routine and trying to find out – in my own interpretation – what my life is all about, whatever the cost. I'll stop at nothing to achieve it.'

'Is this the new morality?'

'New? It's the only one that will enable me – perhaps us, the English – to survive at all. Otherwise we won't be of any use to the future.'

'Are we still talking about the Dinner Service?'

'I'm talking in a manner that would have struck me as idiotic a few weeks ago, when I hadn't seen even a glimpse of the bloody plates.'

'You're obsessed,' said Zinzendorf, with satisfaction.

'I hope so.'

'But only with history.'

'No, not history. Not the past. Look at those works of art. They're alive now. That's the point. Call them history and all you're saying is that history is alive and we can have it back – to relive it, properly, to the full. I think it's a way of destroying time.'

'Is that your final conclusion?'

'Not yet. But you have to reach some conclusion. However apparently temporary. Whatever the consequences.'

'And you'd die for that?' he asked mischievously.

'I don't have to. It's making me more alive every minute.'

'Oh, that's just the pleasure of talking to me.'

'How arrogant. No wonder you're dying. Or dead.'

Zinzendorf laughed. We both laughed.

'Then take it,' he said.

'Take it?'

'Certainly. Take my property down from the wall. Pack it. I'll provide the paper and string. Drink a last brandy with me. And return to England with it.'

Zinzendorf was serious. We were both serious. After a pause I said, 'I can't do that.'

'Why not? You're my guest. You therefore have obligations.'

'I think,' I said, 'that on the whole I'd prefer to steal the pieces from you.'

'As a moral test of your obsession? Yes, I understand that. It's a game, but I see the point. A gift is no challenge, is it? Too patronising. There has to be a fight. You want me to hate you.'

'I want you to be angry that you have lost something of value, yes. I want you to feel your loss.'

'It's very perverse,' Zinzendorf said.

'Obsession doesn't have to answer a comment like that. It creates its own standards.'

He paused. 'I think you are right,' he said. 'You are very like me.' Outside the windows the afternoon light was dying. He moved away. To switch on a light? No, he stood at the door.

'Then, if you're not generous enough to take a gift, borrow them for a while. I don't need them. I expect you'll learn by possessing them that you don't need them either. Come and see me when you've finished.'

Zinzendorf left the room. With a shudder I stood alone, unable to move, disliking the room, yet longing to retrieve from its caricature of the past my version of the present.

Dusky furniture reared, seemed to topple, steadied itself. I picked my way from one item to the next, knocking off a marble surface of small bronze, which fell with the thump of a fist on a door. My heart leapt.

By now I couldn't see what images were racked on the wall. And I thought – an infuriating thought, not grateful at all – how far I had come for so little and, worse, how mean the ethics I was embracing compared to those which the Dinner Service in its magnitude urged me to pursue.

I loathed not earning or paying for these pieces. It devalued them.

There remained only one escape from this dilemma.

Action. An irreversible act.

To lift the pieces down from another man's wall, Lundy first or perhaps it was Skomer, to place them one by one with care one on top of another, St Paul's settling into Southend Pier slipped with a clatter on to the mines of Ebbw Vale, and carry them, the fish-quays at Hull wobbling over the Gothic outlines of a college at Aberystwyth, the bosky suburb of Clapham overlaying Glasgow's massed black streets, and carry them through the twilit passages of German history that kept standing in my way – the top two plates slithering, sandbanks off Kent, a cloister, my spare hand coming up smartly to support them – carry them out into the little daylight that remained, and stand panting.

The woods had gone to sleep. One star showed. Out to sea a lamp went on blinking. I still stood breathing hard, knees bent, my hands perilously sliding under the load of plates. And all my mind could do, bereft at last of any ethical consideration, was to wonder how on earth I could reach my hired car, fifty yards away, with such a burden already slipping through my fingers.

I solved the problem without panache. Lowered these layers of England, my legs wobbling, into the shadow of a bush by the white gate. My lungs rasped. Then I fetched the car, beginning to doubt my luck.

But half England was still there to greet the returning hero. The plates under the shrub leaning slightly sideways – a folly ill-constructed by a fool, a pagoda of pleasures in store. Slowly I picked the whole lot up and stacked it on the floor under the back seat in equal piles. Then waited to be suffused by an overwhelming sense of triumph.

Nothing happened. So I entered the house again. Zinzendorf was ready with more schnapps.

'Have you guessed why?' he said.

'If it's not generosity, no.'

'Then I've come further than you. As I said, we're travellers on the same road.'

'Are you making a mystery of it?'

'It is a mystery,' Zinzendorf said. 'Let me know your findings in due course.'

An hour later, no wiser, I drove into the ferry terminal at Puttgarten.

I had listed my next step. To chase up one Morten Sverdrup, a high functionary at Tivoli before the war. Probably dead. But what had happened to his imposing array of the Dinner Service, which Cyril Fentiman had been shown in 1939? And had mentioned with delight in his notes?

The ferry left for Denmark at midnight. I had fifty minutes to spare.

I wanted to ring up Sophie. And tell her all.

Instead I rang up Humphrey Booth, to thank him.

'So you've turned up,' he said grudgingly. 'Where are you?'

I told him.

'That puts me in a quandary. I suppose I should report your presence.'

'Who to?'

'Oh, London's been bothering me about you,' he said rattily. 'It's most unfair. You never told me you weren't working for those Arts people, what's his name? Ranston.'

'You never asked me.'

'And now they've put me on the line. I'm supposed to help persuade Bonn to cooperate in lending this blasted Dinner Service from museums. You're in the soup, old boy, I can tell you that. They're out for blood.'

'Who are?'

'These arty wallahs. Shouldn't be surprised if they didn't lynch you in the Café Royal or wherever they hang out now. Anyway, why Copenhagen?'

I told him.

'Look, why don't you see my friend Mogens Rald?' Booth said. 'He knows about all this and he's expecting to hear from you. I alerted him before I heard about the official stance. Nice chap.'

'How do you know him?'

'Gave him a hand with some potty art film here in Hamburg. Talkative sod. He mentioned some story about plates getting broken during the war. Thought it might interest you.'

'Why are you doing all this for me?'

'Because I'm a bloody fool,' Booth said with glum humour. 'And I detest the FO interfering. They don't know what goes on abroad. Local customs are a closed book mostly. When you've been as long in the service as I have, you know it's better to keep as much as possible under your hat . . .'

Cold air blew from the north as more sleeping-cars were shunted into the bowels of the boat. It was after midnight. Standing on deck in a squall of sleet, I felt poised on the far edge of the continent. Fur-wrapped businessmen were leaning at the rail as the fat vessel eased out of harbour. And boomed into the rough of the Baltic.

Never again would I willingly set foot in Germany. I had taken what I wanted from her and left behind a void.

Yet what had I gained?

Gulls keened alongside in icy transience – more actual than any achievement of mine. A gush of litter – beercans, old loaves, fish-heads – swung out of a galley and landed with a splosh, birds dived with a shriek. A drama that instantly mattered, then swept past.

What had I gained?

Out of Germany I had collected thirty or so views of my

native country painted on one of the most delicate substances ever devised for art. That was all I had gained. And in the rubbish pouring out of the ship, in this ominous sea roaring me darkly northward away from the spring, in the pad of feet diminishing as those orderly men went below to their sleep, I couldn't see that any of my efforts was worth the struggle.

By now I might have hoped to understand my addiction to those plates. At the deeper or different levels implied by their remote beauty. I ought to have captured a hint of their meaning. Or a subtler reason for their existence than the mere fact of it. But as I lunged towards Denmark I was still at a loss.

Downstairs in the big saloon, to my amazement, stood a buffet. A few men hung over it, forks poised. Bulkheads groaned.

And suddenly there was no point in thinking – making plans – striving to deepen experience.

Here was richness. I dipped into bowls of herring, creamed, spiced, sauced, I spooned up shrimps, I fished slivers of salmon, smoked, marinated, poached, from a succession of dishes, I tried varieties of sardine, anchovy, sprat. With timeless placidity, not tired at all, in a limbo of devastating appetite, I then sat by myself at a table conveying this monumental pile of food into my system. I ordered an iced beer, then another, and tots of icier schnapps. It seemed that only cramming my body with the fruits of the sea could consume doubt or bewilderment.

A nocturnal banquet. From which I now sat back. Wiping my mouth with a paper napkin printed in Germany. Straining into the porthole for a sign of Denmark. Thinking with no coherence at all, but much love, of England.

In Copenhagen next morning I stepped out of the car into hard northern air – touched by scents of cinnamon and coffee – and saw snow falling in such large flakes that it blurred the city's edges into a muffled silence that looked like the past. Even trams only murmured.

I called Mogens Rald from a hotel foyer. At once – in a light tenor lilt – he said, 'I'll take you to breakfast, sir, a Danish breakfast, wait for me ten minutes only, the hotel will seat you, they are friends of mine . . .'

And within five minutes a small figure, fit and trim, buttoned into a fur coat, swung through the doors on hasty tiptoe. And approached me with a grin of excessive delight on his face.

'Aaaaah!' he said.

Cocky, diminutive, full of charm, Mogens Rald greeted me as if I had just liberated Denmark from boredom.

He at once rejected the hotel as 'a mausoleum of our Danish pomposity.'

By the time we were ensconced in a busy café across the street, I knew that for any help my quest needed here I was home and dry. Unless Danes were even more obliquely hypocritical than I was.

We had soft-boiled eggs, toast unctuous with butter, several cups of light coffee that for once tasted like its smell, and – 'to keep our minds up' – a minute but blistering cold inch of Aalborg.

Rald raised his glass. 'To us, whoever we are, wherever we go, whatever we seek, and for all time,' he said – with glimmers of the smile that kept entering his sentences like wit or a double meaning. His energy was immense, but so tiring that I wished I had it.

'I make films, I know everyone, I'm creative,' he said, a hand on my arm. 'This is not boasting, but our way of saying here in Denmark that I will do anything for you.'

He glanced at his digital watch.

'I am one minute late for shooting a quintet of wind. We can speak more at the studios. I have been warned of your approach and I have much to say about the German plates. I was here, you see – a small boy in the war.'

A Volvo awaited us in the snow, engine running to keep up

the heat, driven by a pert girl called Benni, who caught my eye lewdly in the mirror as I sat with Mogens Rald listening to the saga of his current documentary. Gothically unending red-brick castellations of inner suburb whizzed past.

Rald was at work on a film designed to make Denmark sit up and be once more proud of her heritage.

To the east an almost ebony sea slapped a long shore under the white of the snow. 'Over there is Sweden,' Rald said dismissively. I stared. Could see nothing. But felt my wits slip into contentment.

Rald was now developing his theory that films were not made – no, they happened. Nothing, as in life, must be planned. I appeared to have abandoned myself to some process irrelevant to the immediate search for the Dinner Service. A fantasy that might or might not lead to a promised land.

But did this matter? There was time for everything, even spontaneity.

We entered a brightly lit studio to the gusty discords of Carl Nielsen in the hands of five peppery men tuning up. Benni winked.

This morning's sequence was so carefully unplanned as to seem chaotic. 'Nielsen expresses all Europe,' Rald said, turning aside to a bassoonist whose expenses were still unpaid. Round the studio stood tall men wrapped tightly into expensive overcoats as though protecting their wallets, one a surly American who had just flown in. Thought he was in Norway. Had been seconded into PR by a Franco-Italian company with as yet undelivered money in the film.

'The name of the game is forget it,' he muttered, as the quintet, eyes goggling at an outsize screen, plodded through a windy variation. This accompanied shots of men in aprons releasing niagaras of lager into vats – this in turn intercut with dissolves of imported wine being consumed in a student tavern in Roskilde where the Danish kings were buried.

'Jesus,' whispered the American through half-closed eyes,

falling back on his jetlag. The music hooted and brayed to a stop.

'I'm making no moral point,' Rald announced at large. 'Only a human one.'

The quintet sat back, flicking spittle out of their instruments.

In the momentary lull Rald took me aside. 'I shall tell you more later,' he said. 'But during the war I rescued your Dinner Service from the Germans, who were shooting it to pieces for their sport. Remind me please to talk of a man named Sverdrup.'

Recalling Fentiman's notes I said, 'I think I know who you mean.'

'I doubt it. Sverdrup was a traitor to the Danish people.'

The lights flooded up. 'Now we shall shoot,' he called to the camera crew, 'and afterwards ask questions.'

The American bit his lower lip. 'This boy's got something,' he mumbled. 'But I sure as hell don't know what it is.'

One or two false starts ensued. Rald loudly claimed to like them – they were natural. Benni stood very close behind me, breathing. Her skin exuded an odour of slightly over-used bedrooms. She too seemed to be making a human rather than a moral point.

Now Rald retreated into another botched rehearsal. But as the morning ached on, in fits and starts, his war story emerged. Instalments of a serial just as bizarre as the snap happenings in that studio.

In 1944 Colonel Ilsebach was an overpromoted SS youth given to scorn and thin smiles. Throughout the hostilities he had done quiet business with Sverdrup. A few gentlemanly dealings in priceless art. For which the Colonel had paid with a few rather more priceless favours, such as protection from murder and want.

So Sverdrup felt safe. Before the war he was an overseer at Tivoli, counting gate money behind the scenes. Now for three years he had been seduced by the allure of the occupying power and had no intention of paying the penalty.

Quietly over dinner – at his privileged flat – Sverdrup planned to offer Ilsebach his collection of well over 50 pieces of the Imperial German Dinner Service. These he had picked up, together with much else of value, from the sacked homes of undesirables deported to the fatherland. Or from museums whose directors were under arrest.

The Colonel would acknowledge this gift not only as a compliment to his taste, but as Sverdrup's passport to Germany, where the Dinner Service rightly belonged. 'He knew that Denmark would soon be free,' Rald said, 'and we would kill him. Excuse me a moment . . .'

Another hush fell in the studio.

The moment was ready for a final unplanned happening – chance was being given its last opportunity before lunch.

The liquid images – of students in their cellars, workmen pouring beer into vats – passed across the screen, as that huddle of five men under the lights, at the last gasp of their patience, played through the Nielsen Quintet without pause or error.

And I couldn't keep my eyes off the music.

Out of this blind studio the music conjured some melodious farm standing four-square in a surround of echoing hills. The long stride of its phrases penetrated the woodland that seemed full of myths and suddenly put up birdsong in a harmony that tamed nature. In rough weather the tunes crossed to the many islands lying out to sea and brought them beautifully into the scope of my feeling.

I couldn't guess what others thought, as this metallic pure evocation of a country passed through my ears into vision. But in the end, on the last chord, we all clapped. I had never heard music that so gathered together the broken and distributed pieces of my understanding.

'You have that applause on tape?' Rald snapped to the recordist. 'It's real.'

The horn-player shook some gob out of his mouthpiece.

'Christ,' said the American.

It was lunchtime.

I had an open sandwich in the canteen. 'That is a Danish open sandwich,' Rald said, reaching over to validate my anchovies with his fork. He was chewing meatballs rather fast.

'Where was I?' he asked.

'Sverdrup had just invited this German officer to dinner.'

'I know – but he didn't come alone. He was joined by two fellows from the SS, all good companions.'

'Their names?'

He bridled. 'Do you doubt me?'

'I just wondered if you knew.' One of them might have been Zinzendorf. That would not only account for his collection, but relieve my guilt over accepting it.

'I know everything except their names,' Rald said, pursuing the story.

These men sat in idle postures on the arms of Sverdrup's chairs. They drank lukewarm aquavit by candlelight – the Resistance had cut off the electricity. They spoke arrogantly of defeat. Ilsebach was wholly silent. Sullen. On the lookout for some gesture of protest before being ordered back to Germany, routine, shame.

Sverdrup then placed on the flickering table, in front of each guest, three or four plates that bore representations of the heritage that belonged – even if the Kaiser had brought it to birth as art – to their soon to be victorious enemy. And the young Colonel, seeing his chance, chose to regard this hospitality as a calculated insult to both his uniform and the Reich.

According to Rald, the whole scenario gathered spontaneously in his mind. He took one vicious look at the plates, on which food had yet to be served. Then, with a blow of his fist, he shattered Rochester and Chatham. Sharp edges of cathedrals and naval barracks adhered briefly to the fleshy hand. Sverdrup's mouth sagged.

Ilsebach next used the butt of a fork to crack a side-plate with an unusual view of Bangor on it, and while Sverdrup goggled, as if recognising the value of art only when he was losing it, another officer picked up a Scottish loch and hurled it against the wall. A spray of spilt beer sizzled into a candle, darkening the room's mood.

Ilsebach raised a hand. Stood up, his dress sword clanking in its scabbard. 'Wait,' he said, 'we shall make public our undying hatred of the enemy. These pieces of England shall be the target of our contempt. Come, gentlemen.' And his fellow officers stood erect among the splinters that littered the furniture.

Mogens Rald paused, then stood, as if imitating the formality of that distant moment. From my open sandwich I dubiously ate a fragment of cold egg half wrapped in a leaf of forced lettuce.

'I didn't know young Nazis admired the Kaiser,' I said. 'Or had swords.'

'There is much you do not know,' Rald said, smiling brilliantly. 'I shall tell it all later, when we have time. Now we must film more reality. Everyone is waiting.'

It was two o'clock. The afternoon's happening was on the point of being spontaneous in Raadhuspladsen, a square crisscrossed by trams. Dominated by a city hall topped by a precarious icing of snow. A wedding cake in a dream.

A statue of Hans Andersen, also capped in white, stood in isolation below a tower which brittly chimed out a childish peal – at intervals that seemed not to correspond to normal time.

The occasion was to be a protest by militant farmers against some policy to do with the short-sighted export of livestock. It struck me as monumentally irrelevant, if not mad. But it was too real to be missed on film. Benni winked.

We drove up behind a series of smelly trailers parked outside Tivoli.

'Over there,' Rald said, as if lying, 'is Tivoli, all foreigners know Tivoli, we Danes love it too, and that is where Ilsebach decreed that the English plates must be set up for his fun.'

He lowered his voice. Spread his hands for dramatic effect. 'It is a spring night in Copenhagen . . .' he whispered.

Behind him a squall of slow snow shifted across some pigs being unloaded from a trailer, under the eye of a policeman in a fur hat. Tivoli had tall iron railings and a few bare trees reaching to the sky. Amid them stood a garishly oriental structure that lacked paint.

German guards were at the gate, Rald said. But Ilsebach had the required authority to enter. The three soldiers marched in and on. Down the empty lanes past a shut theatre. Past a peeling restaurant starved for the duration behind panes of dusty glass. Carrying in their gloved hands the items of the Dinner Service rescued for this escapade from the clutches of a traitor.

Sverdrup walked gauntly, as if in irons, between his protectors. He must have sensed that his life or death were issues in this game, whatever it was . . .

Then Rald said, 'Forgive me,' and ran off.

In the square the trams, drawn up nose to tail, were pouring out crowds of people – who now shuffled and stared at the camera crews dotted under the statues: the crews in turn focusing on a makeshift platform, where several farmers were arguing inaudibly with a battery of microphones that either screeched or went dead.

Rald had snatched a loudhailer. A pig yelped behind me. A dozen hefty porkers snuffled over the pavements in a wide arc, dispersing the bystanders – who suddenly behaved, overcoats flapping, legs treading slush, with just the panic of the beasts they were trying to elude.

Rald lodged a camera against his shoulder. Moved in pursuit.

Filming the disorder as precisely the kind of occurrence that proved his point about the superiority of cinema over reality. Cheap exports cavorted away from him. The future of the bacon trade ran amok.

Nothing of note was happening at this moment. It would only take place later when people saw it on television. Meanwhile the scene was yet another of the illusions. Like mine, over the Dinner Service. Like everyone else's over their private obsessions. An illusion confirmed now by a frieze of tourists lifting instamatics to their faces, taking snaps of the professionals taking pictures of the pigs.

The afternoon light was dying. A grey steady snow fell vertically, ruining proportion, putting the truth out of true. A piglet, overhung by a policeman trying to corner it, nuzzled the base of the more than lifesize statue of Hans Andersen gazing down on this fairytale of an occasion.

Would I ever hear the rest of the facts, if facts they were, about Sverdrup?

Again a mike boomed, echoing back off muffled buildings. The snake of stuck trams clanged their bells in protest against the obstruction.

The whole of Copenhagen seemed to have reached the centre. Just in time for an event that was not quite happening. From the platform a caucus of spokesmen issued half-heard speeches – lending dignity to the notion of democratic colloquy while they engaged in nervous struggle with the electronics.

By now the pigs, the only free agents in sight, had begun to endear their puzzled natures to the onlookers. A well-heeled woman shrieked as a pig, trotting past her ankles, caused her to drop a shopping bag. A hat rolled out and hooped into the muddle. A spritely man in leather gave clownish chase amid applause.

The pigs were winning.

Then a whistle blew. It was Rald.

All the livestock had been caught and returned in outrage to the lorries. The demo was over. Democracy had survived yet another withering assault from the media.

'The only right thing about this,' Rald said sagely, 'is that it all went wrong.' And I still believed in him enough to suspect that even his lies had an illusory truth. Benni winked.

Within minutes the chaos had melted and I was standing, bereft of sense, next to the statue of Hans Andersen. Rald pointed at the slush under the pedestal. Trotters were imprinted on it.

'Imagine the body of this Sverdrup lying there,' he said quietly. 'And the people gathering in the night to look at the remains of a traitor.'

'What had happened?'

'Your plates were stood against a wall, there in Tivoli, which is sacred to the Danish love of pleasure,' Rald said.

I looked through the bleak air to the skyline of follies just visible behind the iron fence.

With their revolvers the three German officers, at a hundred paces, making it none too easy for their marksmanship, picked off, one after another, the remaining pieces of the Dinner Service, taking their time to reload, ordering Sverdrup to dash out of cover, cringing, and set in position the plates they had only chipped or marginally damaged. All this was carried out with impeccable discipline.

In blacked-out flats, at that late hour, local ears listened with only small surprise to the crack of execution down there in the gardens.

Nobody disturbed the slaughter. The heart of Bradford was destroyed by a single bullet. Market halls tumbled with a smash as their glass roofs caved in. Whole terraces of the eighteenth century fell into the gorge of the Avon at Clifton. While, a few inches away, propped against the boarding of a once exclusive restaurant, the Fens were flattened by two almost simultaneous shots. Ely Cathedral was sliced in half. And so it went on, until much of England lay in splinters on the grass.

'You seem to know your landmarks,' I said.

'I have not yet told you all,' Rald said with a glimmer of reproach.

The largest plate had been kept till last.

It was a serving dish that displayed in unblemished detail the Inns of Court. Flanked by the two SS officers, Sverdrup was instructed to hold the Middle Temple, the alleys, the chapels, the forums of law, in front of his face like a blindfold, while Colonel Ilsebach – with more care now – savouring the precision of his aim – fired.

Only once.

The traitor's head shattered into fragments of ceramic, and he fell among the ruins of such parts of the enemy country as he had preserved as his insurance against death. His last sight, if he could focus, must have been of the word Wedgwood and the date 1914. A jagged bit of chambers had penetrated the mush of his eye.

The two SS men, at Ilsebach's command, carried the body out into the public square beyond Tivoli. And threw it at the feet of Hans Andersen, where we now stood. This act, in Rald's view, was the debt paid by an honourable foe to a nation which this victim of his own greed had betrayed.

'That is not just how I see it,' Rald said. 'It is how it is.'

It was now quite dark. Trotters were melting in the snow where Sverdrup's corpse had been slung. Water dripped off the stony face of the fabulist. I moved away, puzzled by disbelief. Rald's story had access to too many hard facts to be credible.

'How do you know all this?' I said.

Patiently Rald sighed. It was very simple. He and his young friends, brave juniors of the Resistance, had been spying on Ilsebach's fun and games between the chinks in the shutters of a nearby shooting gallery, their headquarters. With glee they had seen Sverdrup's body borne into outer darkness. They had picked up all the pieces, taken them home – and, in the intervals between blowing up lorries and firing oil-tanks, put them together again.

Here the plot thickened almost to opacity. Night after night these boys had sat at home in the blackout – a further note of reproach in Rald's voice – mending my native country. So that when Ilsebach and his vile crew departed for good the pieces he had tried to destroy could be restored to their rightful owner.

'Who was that?'

'Nobody claimed them,' Rald said. 'Now they are all over Copenhagen. Tonight we shall find them together. Then at dawn we shall be shooting in Tivoli – for you have given me this idea for my film . . .'

It was a long night. Always time to visit yet another bar. To reach a party at its peak – at any one of which Rald's crew, thrown together only by the reality of film, passed into ever more hazy sleazy relations with one another. We would all be dead by morning. So now a lifetime must be crammed into the small hours.

Very soon pickled we drifted along bare streets, lunging at displays of goods in windows. Picked up unknown people. Dropped them, seeing them disappear in fast taxis. Only to turn up somewhere else in the city a while later with more wine, another identity. And Benni always there, pouting, not saying much, and I wondered where I was, and how close we were to the Dinner Service.

Halfway through that night I was genuinely believing it to be a silly happy sketch for a whole life. Wind music entered into it, and the police being asked to chase pigs elsewhere, and men being shot, and shrimps caught on local littorals, and beef ground into tartare with yolks on top, and wine being slopped in cellars that smacked of student conspiracy.

And Benni always there, now and then smiling at me through the smoke, winking.

Being distantly aware of Mogens Rald asking some shadowy

face a question, no doubt trying to round up the Dinner Service for me. At times nodding encouragement. And then we moved on again.

That night had no sequence. Cause and effect were wickedly hidden behind the apparent inevitability of what happened next. Yet there was always a cause, and I soon realised it was Mogens.

He had manipulated the entire day into being – this self-appointed demigod in the neat bow-tie, who couldn't bear anything to happen unless he had arranged it. This cold fish who put up such a front of warmth.

Mogens was a delight that evening, purveying his elegance in other people's premises. Yet he meant none of it. His gaiety was all bounce. His life was nowhere near the bubbling surface. His life lay in some icy depth which – as I watched him perform, tickle others with his charm – felt like grief. I understood that within he was mourning a lost element, perhaps of himself. Wishing, even willing, the dawn to bring tragedy, a death in the dirty waters of Nyhavn, with everyone else in the party too absorbed in drink or sex to be capable of mounting a rescue. Still less of filming it.

And I understood all that as if it were me. Or me yesterday. Or me before I started on the Dinner Service.

Six in the morning, taste of dead beer in my mouth, Benni caressing my fingertips. Yes, a nightmare contrived by the depressed mischief of Mogens Rald, and a loosening of my own mind's hold on reality.

The farce of the Dinner Service being smashed to bits made no sense in this extremity of fatigue, as a slow grubby dawn touched the brickwork of the city with the hues of dried blood. And the domes lifted as snowy as onions against the leaden skyline. And spires were coppered by a glimmer of sun.

It looked like fantasy, conjured out of the hat by Rald, a man as hopeless as I was before I began the search.

* * *

Shortly after 7 a.m. we arrived at Tivoli. The haunt of pleasure was deserted at that hour, but Rald had the keys to everything.

While cameras were set up he unlocked the booth where in summer visitors released their aggressions by hurling balls at reject china. This was no more than an enlarged sentrybox with narrow shelves to lodge the plates. The scene needed no clarification, said Rald. It merely existed. It happened to be happening now, and an audience could make of it what fun or misery they liked.

That was art.

Benni bent to pick up a stone. She and I were to serve as unseen extras in this extravaganza of destruction.

'Are there no balls?' Rald said querulously.

There were no balls. He fingered his bunch for the right key.

'You can't break these plates without the right balls,' he said.

Benni turned on me a fierce glance. 'Come,' she said, 'let us look for these balls,' and in a quickening light, a foreglow sharply printing the city on the eastern horizon, I followed her behind the shy to a storeroom. It was piled to the roof with seconds, dinner-plates sliding in their hundreds out of cardboard boxes, unglazed, their dull faces carrying no image or association – and here our lips touched, just once, with so spinal a quiver that I recoiled, as if repelled, short of breath. Wanting more. There were no balls.

Benni picked up an armful of plates. They clattered in her arms. Outside Rald's voice called action. She grinned.

In a moment, with care, taking aim, I was throwing stones at the array of faceless plates in the booth, hurting my shoulder. With a hint of beery pain over my left eye. But noticing Benni with a flick of the wrist scoring far more accurately.

My shots went wilder. I chipped plates without shifting them. No grand crash excited me into an appetite for greater success. I kept missing. I blamed the camera lens on me, I blamed my form, my age, I silently appealed against bad light.

But for the life of me I couldn't bring down a single one of those plates. And this seemed to matter.

Then Rald called cut. He had what he wanted. Benni threw one more stone and struck a plate in the middle and shattered it. She looked at me with admiration.

'It should have been balls,' Rald said. Tapping my shoulder in apology for a happening which by his standards had never properly occurred.

'By the way,' I said, 'have you managed to find any of the pieces? You did say . . . but perhaps this is the wrong moment to ask.'

'No moment is wrong. Each moment has an authority of its own.' He looked at me coldly, as if I had ceased to exist. Perhaps I had failed his wavelength or tried for too much reality. 'But give me your address in England. I will then write when I have something to say to you.'

'My impression was that you hoped to be finding one or two of the plates during the night.'

'Ah, alas, no. But go, if you are interested, to Tjustvik in Sweden. The people there do make fine china and are friends of mine. I shall telephone them now.'

'Have you nothing for me?'

'Not at present.'

'Can't you do better than that?'

'As I say, I shall telephone my friends at once.'

Rald shrugged. All energy drained out of him. He glanced down at my hand, which Benni was holding tight – I had only just realised it. He cast a deeply sardonic look at the girl and shrugged again. Her grip tightened.

'Benni will tell you all you need to know in bed,' Rald said with scorn. 'I hope we have done all we can to make you at home in Denmark.'

And he walked off towards his car, as a first shaft of sunlight flickered through the bitter trees.

'He is in love with me,' Benni said with a giggle.

'I didn't know.'

'Forget it,' she said.

I forgot it. Indeed my tired brain didn't really register it. I put an arm round her, I felt warmly chilled by the acres of the square, we tripped past Hans Andersen, we strutted in unison down a sinuous street of shut shops, our footsteps echoed back off churches, and a passing tram rattled our teeth.

In my hotel room, where my big haul of the Dinner Service from Germany rested safe and sound, Benni undressed in a trice and I loosened my tie. I wondered what I had forgotten to do. The cleft of Benni's bottom bounced into bed. I followed it, only just remembering that I had meant to ring Sophie and say that I had strayed into a totally mad country and the Dinner Service was all fantasy and shouldn't I forget it?

But the hours of joy that now came, and went on till well past noon, were far beyond fantasy and more incredible.

Sweden. A dull shore. An efficient docking. In the train a compartment of clean dead air. The train picking up speed without a sound, the view passing over ups and downs of landscape so limitless that they denied the passage of time. Immobile weather, not quite snowing out of a constipated sky.

Then, hours later, a tunnel roared. With no hint of suburb we were suddenly crossing bridges. Traversing islands built up into pyramids of dark medieval romance. Passing clusters of streets pulsating with lamplight netted in water – and there I was, in abrupt elation, plunged into the surprise of Stockholm.

The train drew to a halt at a long platform where a handsome woman stood.

Apologies for her husband, who was busy, took us to the car. Light criticism of him lasted the short journey out to the factory. Gunilla Lanzelius had a sharp avian mouth designed for sarcasm, a beak that bit into language. Her silences seemed to be preparing veiled insults. We arrived at a tall wooden house with a spire, a curlicued veranda, and all the lights on.

I said that she had a beautiful home.

She said that on the contrary this was their guest-house.

I said how lucky I was to be offered a room amid such luxury.

She said that I had the place to myself.

The undercurrents of this courtly dialogue suggested a shared amusement at the expense of her husband whom I had yet to meet.

A glass door on the veranda, a wave of silent heat. Before I could focus on the homespun amenities – rose-pink, baby-blue, lit in amber – my two suitcases heavy with the Dinner Service were preceding me upstairs. Carried by a hefty shape with a swaying topknot of honey-blond hair.

'My name is Katinka,' said the girl. 'You can ask me for anything. You have one hour and the bathroom is here and you would like a drink after your long journey.'

She had full lips on which a posed smile was painted, eyes very steady. In a moment I heard water running and saw steam ballooning round her bent shape. I raised my eyes to the bedroom ceiling. It had seraphs at the corners blowing trumpets towards the four-poster.

Ten minutes later a light knock. 'Here is your drink,' she said, dissolving backwards into the steam. The tray bore an iced jug of martini and some hot pastry snacks in which creamy prawns skulked. I lay in the bath becoming sozzled and happy and unpunctual.

I was a few minutes late for dinner at the main house.

'Ah,' Lanzelius said. 'It does not matter one bit that you are late. Everything is arranged.'

He shook my hand.

'Come and be seated,' he said, indicating a basket chair under a canopy of glass, through which I saw blurred stars. He moved heavily among exotic shrubs, brushing off an orchid bloom with the edge of his jacket. It was hotter than the bath.

Tall, brusque, thick lips on the move as if dictating, Rolf Lanzelius now quoted in full a letter he had received from

Courtney Ranston, asking for his help. 'Yes, the Dinner Service,' he said with an air of reflection that presaged tedium. 'Ah, but you would like a drink after your long journey.'

He snapped his fingers towards cooler areas of the house. A small green lizard zipped over a leaf and ogled me steadily, tail in air. It looked preserved.

Gunilla Lanzelius entered almost promptly. An iced jug of martini, three glasses.

She said that she had been just about to bring in the drinks.

He said that their guest, after his long journey, had unhappily been kept waiting for his drink.

Drinks were poured in silence.

Dinner was served in a perfect dining-room. An evening of perfect manners ensued. Glasses were raised, at strictly correct moments – creating an abysmal pause just when talk was flowing, just when an awkward moment ebbed.

Gunilla told me, her lips biting the compliment to shreds, how beautiful the Dinner Service was.

And how well she understood the nature of my emotional involvement.

And how much she would like – if only her husband demanded less of her time as the factory's publicity chief – to help me in my search.

Lanzelius, eyes protruding, stared at her bitterly over his wine.

He then told me that, though he personally had no intention of releasing without good reason such pieces of the Dinner Service as were still in his possession, his wife had once kindly made the acquaintance of an English fisherman, who had taken a fancy to a very large dish which bore a rather important picture of King's College, Cambridge. She had loaned this dish to the English fisherman, who had at once vanished into Iceland never to return.

'He is dead,' said Lanzelius.

In the gloom Gunilla lightly tapped her glass.

'Oh,' Lanzelius said with an enraged smile, lifting his brandy in yet another regulation toast. 'We are pleased to entertain in our home a guest who shares our deeply felt interests. It is not often in Sweden . . .'

His sentences began to thicken. From the folds of his jacket he produced a slip of typed paper.

'Here,' he said, 'is your programme for tomorrow.'

'If he survives tonight,' Gunilla said acidly.

Dinner was over. And I was half-dead with fatigue. And longing for Sophie.

Why? Why now? I felt knocked out by a horror I had never noticed before – the self-indulgence of hatred. Those two people lived off their poison. It ran in their veins with the pleasure of a drug. They were feeding on a species of emotional pornography.

Yes, I noticed it – and I hated it. Neither of them was capable of love, because each thought the other grotesquely unloving. And I saw myself and Sophie in them, in the same corrupt trap of ego.

I longed for her.

No wonder wider wars occurred, when two people living together were entangled in the politics of such detestation. And I saw in a flash that the Dinner Service's poignancy lay in showing the world as it was in that innocence of time before the big wars took place.

Only inside me could the world be like that again. And it would.

I phoned home from the guest-house. Sophie was out.

My programmed visit to the factory's museum was conducted by Lanzelius almost at a trot. A small pavilion walled in sheets of glass gave the country outside the washed-out look of amateur art. The exhibits – a century's production in glass and earthenware – were housed in oblong glass cases as if in a mortuary of transparent coffins.

I listened to a potted history of the firm. Which Gunilla kept correcting. Only to have her corrections questioned on points of detail. Which Gunilla said were trifling.

Then we were gazing down at three plates.

Lanzelius said, as though springing a surprise, that these plates belonged to the Imperial German Dinner Service. They were particularly fine examples, he said. He said that he would now describe the pictures that adorned them. They were of English landmarks, he said. The one in the middle . . .

His voice faded off. I was confronted by the chapel quad of my school as it was in 1914. There was the mullioned window behind which the headmaster in my day ate chocolate biscuits and wielded a cane at the slightest offence. Pre-war boys, soon to die, were busy keeping off the grass and avoiding the pathway reserved for prefects.

The shadow of the tower indicated that it was about four o'clock on a summer afternoon. The backing of trees by the cricket field was thirty years less tall than when I was there. I had been unknowingly happy.

I looked up. Gunilla's round blue eyes were on me. She bit her lip, then nodded.

What had she seen?

Lanzelius turned. He said that the picture on the left showed Hythe – it was actually Rye – a small sea-port of yesteryear imbued with the medieval charm in which my country was still so rich. And here I was, for a whole curtained day and night, muttering and giggling in a hotel bedroom with linenfold panels and a slanting floor, ignoring literary echoes and teashops and every attraction outside – and making love at intervals to Sophie. We had just met. I wanted to spend my life with her.

And, as I glanced up again, Gunilla seemed aware of this fact. Her face was tense. Broody.

What had she seen?

Lanzelius turned. He said that the plate on the right illustrated Covent Garden, the market famous for . . . He was again mistaken. Men with flat hats were hurrying boxes of fish on their heads across the cobbles from high-sided carts. And I glimpsed the corner stall just inside the portal where on winter mornings in the damp light of Billingsgate – I still missed it – I used to bargain for a week's supply of kippers.

Now they had closed the market. It existed only on a plate.

I sighed. Gunilla had a neat knowing smile. What had she seen? That I was chilled by seeing the Dinner Service on formal display?

At least I knew why I couldn't bear the thought of Courtney Ranston winning. Like this man, he was all show. The art was on the surface. It didn't matter a hoot what was being displayed, as long as it was set off to best advantage – and solemnly discussed as if it existed only in the past.

Looking at me with a touch of satisfaction, Lanzelius said that on no account could he allow me to touch or handle the items in the glass case, not at least until we had established at leisure the wishes of the British authorities.

I nodded. Gunilla pouted. Lanzelius led the way.

The next event on my programme was luncheon. Dread suffused me at the thought of yet again sitting down to lengthy refreshment. Of listening to marital violence disguised as courtesy. Of maintaining the lie about my role in the search for the Dinner Service.

And I loved Sophie. I realised that I did love Sophie. By now she would be laughing her head off.

But Lanzelius was late for lunch. He phoned the house, with regrets, to instruct us to drink a glass of sherry in his absence. I looked at Gunilla. She met my eye without humour – but with a blend of compassion and challenge.

We drank a glass of sherry each.

I said I had something to confess to her.

'You looked at those pieces like a man in love,' she said sharply. 'Are you in love?'

I said yes, I was in love with the pieces.

'You know of course that my husband does not value what he possesses. He only values owning it.'

'That doesn't help me.'

'Nor me.'

She smirked.

I said I wasn't working for the Government or for anyone else.

'You behave as if you represent nothing but yourself,' she said. 'It shows. That is why I say you're in love.'

She looked at me firmly. I wished she were less unhappy – but could explain nothing to her. Nothing of the Dinner Service. Still less of Sophie. Then an outside door opened softly, closed with a bang. 'Things could not be worse than they are,' she said chattily, as Lanzelius entered the room in business suiting.

I was soon to know why he had been late.

First he permitted luncheon to pursue its slow course.

Over herring he said that he did not comprehend the meaning behind such English proverbs as letting sleeping dogs lie, though he responded to the traditional English notion that familiarity bred contempt.

Gunilla said that all proverbs, like much of life, enshrined the ideas which we liked to believe were true.

I said that it was a pity that we couldn't live without crutches.

Crutch? Lanzelius asked what a crutch was.

I explained that it was something that supported people who had lost the use of a vital part.

Then Lanzelius said, 'I now know that you are here under false pretences.'

'He is not the only one,' Gunilla said, leaving the room, her napkin floating to the floor.

For the next ten minutes Lanzelius didn't look at me once. He told the middle distance that I was not what I seemed. Through a window he addressed a garden shrunk by winter on the subject of a letter received that morning from Mr Ranston in England, who really did represent the desires of my Government, to the effect that I didn't. Drawing this letter from his pocket, Lanzelius quoted it at length to the remains of the cheese. Then after a pause he politely asked the polished table, when I had finished my coffee, to leave his home.

We did not shake hands.

Why did I then feel gloriously free?

I had failed the Dinner Service, perhaps myself, but the air outside was clean, if not springlike. Katinka had left my packed bags on the verandah. The taxi smelt of hot luxury. Within a few minutes I was purring downhill towards a complicated cut-out of Stockholm on all her islands, blackening against a red sunset. And I still felt free. Why had I always found it so hard to admit that I loved Sophie – and wanted her to be here, and share, and muddle on, and titter, and quarrel, and join in, and shout, and spend night after night in bed dreaming of things like the Dinner Service? And I still felt free.

A little sports car, buzzing about behind, manoeuvring between tram-lines, outpaced my driver. Flagged us down.

Gunilla stepped out. Wrenched open my door. Grinned feebly. Threw a formidable parcel on to the upholstery.

It was a wooden box, tight-wrapped in thick paper, tensely strung and sealed.

I looked at it. In the background views of Stockholm were framed like postcards in the windscreen. In the box were unseen bits of England.

Gunilla waved me off. She said, 'I hope we meet.'

'I hope you have no trouble.'

'That's my only excitement,' she said, blowing a kiss off scornful lips.

From the station I phoned home. Sophie was in, but going out.

I told her where I was. I said I was going to Iceland.

'Go to Paris,' she said.

'Why?'

'An ex of mine, an art-dealer – you remember Philippe Guin?

He saw my bit in the paper. He's found half Bournemouth and some other dishy dishes. Wouldn't you like to have them?

'Why are you telling me this? I thought . . .'

'It's called a volte-face, darling. All details later. Are you getting anywhere?'

'Yes. How's the official search going?'

'Too well. That's why I want you to balance things up a bit. When are you coming home? I miss you.'

'When I've been to Iceland.'

'And Paris. Urgent. Courtney's on to it.'

'I miss you.'

'Good,' said Sophie. 'I'm glad you're away because I don't like it. I'm glad you're doing something because I hate being the only one.'

'Any more definitions of love?'

'Golly, I must go, it's late . . .'

I overpaid the taxi-driver, who complained, mentioned the police, called the whole of Paris to witness – until Philippe Guin strode off to a dark door in a block of seedy flats. The métro grinding overhead on a viaduct. A deserted café on the corner with one table outside.

Guin pushed open the door, grimily paned with arabesques of stained glass. Then walked, footsteps echoing, across the empty auditorium of a tall small theatre. Bracketed rows of plush seats were heaped at angles. One balcony after another towered upwards to a dome of much-faded glass in the roof.

'I have bought it,' Guin said.

The stage was a medley of badly executed backcloths for shows long gone. Streets in Montmartre, gardens in Vienna, crumpled canvases of the Tower of London, avenues of lime-trees in the Balkans. Much of two-dimensional Europe shredding off the frames, scattering scales of tired paint.

'It is all mine,' Guin said with pride, as we penetrated the dank areas behind the stage.

We entered a small room. He switched on a bulb. There was a mirror frosted with dust and distortion. A few costumes hung from pegs. A kepi, a gilded sash, uncreased trousers suspended as from a gibbet, a pike, joke props from the Middle Ages, eighteenth-century high life, a garden in Spain.

With his toe Guin gently kicked a wooden crate that had once contained Italian apples.

'I found the piece here,' he said. 'It told me, because of you, no, because of Sophie, to buy this place for my next gallery. It was the sign I wanted.'

I looked at the apple crate. 'What exactly did you find, Philippe?'

'Ah,' he said. 'I excite you so much that you have missed the point. I found half a dessert plate belonging to the service which you seek.'

A faint reverberation from the métro. Boards trembled underfoot. 'Where is it?'

'But there is more.'

'Where is it?'

Down a passage, up three flights of breathless stairs. Guin tapped at a loose door that swung open. A tiny man in a vest and baggy sky-blue trousers ran forward as if making an entrance.

'Here,' said Guin, 'is the funniest comic in Paris and this theatre was the scene of his many triumphs.'

The little man shook my hand. Bowed. Twirled. And then, widening his mouth into a tragic mask, told at length a joke which Guin considered uproarious.

'So bring them out, master,' Guin said. 'This is the man whose wife I love.'

The comedian trotted to a cupboard and brought out three and a half plates. A mouse ran in a shiver across the floor. On all fours the retired jester laid out his booty on the boards.

There was indeed half of Bournemouth. The wrong half socially. The jagged divide cut through the Royal Bath, roughly where I had sat at lunch with Myra Tremlett. A good part of the pavilion gardens, where in the pines red squirrels squatted on the edge of extinction, was missing.

But the other pieces were flawless.

Oddly enough they were of places I didn't recognise. Were they fakes?

The vine-leaves looked authentic. The eagle stood as beakily hostile as ever. But in the architecture of a country house there seemed an element alien to our island heritage. While a range of hills topped by trees had a remote air that felt storm-tossed, uneasy.

No time to examine them properly – Philippe was haggling. And against me.

'No present for Sophie can be cheap, come now, I must hurry back to the gallery . . .' And he sketched out the circumstances of this wretched comic broken on the tragic wheel of French indifference – its failure of humour – the bourgeois treadmill of its work ethic. The phrases poured over me long after I gave up hope of being let off lightly.

The little man rose from his knees. Pirouetted. Shrugged slyly in an exaggerated mime of poverty. Then thrust out the plates to me on the flat of both hands.

Why not? Let the fellow have my money. It was useless to me without the Dinner Service, false or not. And useless even with it. I just wanted to buy this ludicrous moment, whatever the cost.

I completed several traveller's cheques as if signing autographs.

A few tears welled in the comedian's eyes.

The Gare de Lyon. Night train to Avignon. To Walvish, yes, Walvish, I remembered his name just in time – brother of Hilary Smith, that Cumbrian lady who had lent me the plate of her own house in fragments.

In the train I laid out the pieces on the couchette of a man boarding at Dijon. They rattled dangerously round a curve. I gazed at them almost in the hope of detecting their lack of authenticity.

They had cost 3,000 francs apiece.

The light was dim. The pieces slithered on the sheet. But even so I saw that they were true. It was I in the haste of the moment who had made the mistake of identifying them wrongly. Or had failed to identify them at all.

There was more to England than I knew.

Those windy downs existed as part of the whole, even if I hadn't visited them. As for the house, some foreign influence may have affected the builder's taste, but it was only my limitations that assumed it to be other than English.

It was just a setting I had never seen – without private associations to hinder my judgment or sentimentalise it. Which ought to mean my placing an even higher value on its novelty. As a mystery untapped, an aspect of my country unexplored, a place where things happened differently.

It took me several miles of gathering speed – Melun flashed past in a flurry of suburban lamplight – to tackle the fact that the Dinner Service hadn't been invented merely to indulge my sense of familiarity. The scale was larger than that. However many lies I chose to tell myself, the Dinner Service, either in part or as a whole, even more as a whole, did not lie. Could not.

As I drifted asleep, the carriage bumping over points, I wondered how capable I was of facing up to unfamiliarity. Or must I always think it as false or unnecessary as a prejudice?

I took at once to William Walvish.

He lived alone, if with several servants. In a castle on a mound overlooking a marshy plain ringed by hills of scrub where wild boar roamed.

The castle was all his own work – with a modicum of help from the Middle Ages. He had transformed the ruins of the summer palace of the bishops of Vignargues – walls six foot thick, defences to withstand sectarian attack, slits for windows

– into a place where a man of spirit might live on his own terms.

An achievement of three years that looked centuries old. Even the interior fountains that played among forced vegetation in this courtyard or that seemed to have dribbled there for ever. Without affectation. Fig and oleander flourished with an air of myth. The whole place, looming over the usual terracotta of rustic meridional rooftops in the village below the walls, felt legendary.

Walvish was well over sixty. White hair sprouted off his head. The mistral that morning had blown his valley clear of cloud. The blue sky intensified his eyes.

His big brown mouth, freckled skin, beaked nose, seemed attractively mortal – in their mobility. And he spoke a high-toned English that yanked words out of the air, staccato, his brilliant effect owing more to tone of voice than choice of phrase.

The rooms – lengthened by perspectives of books, dark against the sun – were a repository of valuables. Multitudinous proof of a life lived with a vindictive need to collect it as it passed. Walvish was ravished by possessions, yet only as an outward sign that he was alive. Or so he said.

If they vanished, were stolen – a Dali inscribed to him, letters from Thomas Mann, a sketch Churchill had made of the castle, some signed Cocteaus which looked read – Walvish claimed that he wouldn't mind. Their reality was in him.

For a while I had the satisfactory sense that all my travels, often making me work against my nature or resolving into disappointment, had been drawing me accurately to just this place and time. The middle of the day, in a sudden hot spring. Cool within these protective walls. Somewhere out in the blowy countryside west of Avignon. Vineyards flowing away from the ramparts below us. Time itself not exactly stopping, but pausing for long enough to allow me a rare glimpse in both directions – to the past trapped alive in the long room where we lunched, to the future limitlessly unavoidable beyond it.

I stayed with Walvish for three days. With growing impatience, but unable to move. The weather was too good, the comfort of being immured in privilege. But some tension in the castle's atmosphere began to leave me uneasy. No more than a fingertip of doubt in my stomach. But it nagged.

I could fault none of the arrangements. Walvish was arranging a party for me. Making local enquiries about the Dinner Service. The light was glorious. But I felt that life, in particular French life, was being paraded before me as an ideal – and then fading before I had a chance to live any of it. The meals at that civilised table began to mount up, congest, slacken my mind. The food was so exquisite that I could only pick at it.

I longed to detect a mistake. To climb back on the shaky wagon of comparative values. To find some detail that didn't quite measure up.

Walvish's talk irked me too. 'I like your spunk,' he said at dinner. 'You have taken on a government, well knowing you will fail, but acting, I would say, out of pure hatred.'

'I think not. Indeed I believe the opposite.'

'Love? No, no,' Walvish said. 'You're fighting an opposition of your own choice. You needed one. Love may come into it later, but for the moment you're one of us – loathing mirrors for fear of what you'll see . . .'

All right – no argument. But it was as if none of the burden of culture massed in this castle, the plunder of centuries, well-digested Europe caught in a vacuum of luxury, had made on Walvish's brains more than the most superficial of dints.

The rest was a blank filled with emotion of which he denied the existence. Perhaps he himself was the only mirror in the house, and all it reflected was me.

For then, hearing him on the phone asking yet another local savant what he knew of the Dinner Service, asking whether the Languedoc had any treasure to offer, I heard the tones of my own voice asking those very questions. Detached. Loveless. Cerebral. I began to wish he would leave the Dinner Service alone – hating his fashion of advertising to a personal mafia that he needed help for a passing guest.

Well, yes, I suppose I still wanted to come upon a secret which nobody else had even suspected, let alone sought. Walvish didn't make it easy.

Nothing made it any easier.

On the day of the party the Arab servants flitted with cutlery and glass in and out of the vaulted cellars, where a table was laid for forty.

Walvish had invited everyone. I gathered the entire region wished to meet a man pitting his wits against the state. Even against a prince of the realm. My host kept telling me how distinguished the gathering was to be. As if conjuring out of fantasy an ideal of France that was lost or scattered – until he summoned it to his board.

The guests gathered on an upper terrace backed by a turquoise sky, which gave the women a blush of mystery and the men a shadowy look of high fashion. People posed with their drinks, as for pictures. In those first moments the scene had the spurious grace of page after page of an out-of-date magazine.

They had come at short notice from far and wide. Driving up from the Camargue in florid shirts or down from the Ardèche in a glitter of jewels. Touching my arm with long nails, placing a tanned hand on my shoulder, everyone seemed intent on telling me how marvellous Willie's last party had been. And what a pity I had missed it. And therefore what small chance we had that this occasion would generate the same unique sequence of events.

A countess had danced in a fountain. A modish dress-designer from Avignon had modelled a floodlit boy who had tried to make love to a peacock. A Swiss critic of international repute had worked his wits so hard that he had a stroke. The wet countess had to chase off the peacock, which was nearly run over by the ambulance.

All this animated reminiscence grew so fatiguing that I felt I had been dropped back into the reality of the earlier party – so was missing the point of this one. However, the point – Walvish vaunting me as his latest find – soon struck me, as dusk fell, women shivered, and we withdrew indoors. The point was to honour, criticise, deprecate, gush over, ignore, fail to see the fun in, turn the back on, pour scorn or drink over, and generally make a feature of both the Dinner Service and me.

Me as the brilliant man who fashioned it from clay with his own hands (according to the silly woman who had danced in the fountain). Me as a very rough number cheating his own country of its few remaining possessions (in the view of a voluble expatriate who dragged up an unwilling boy-friend to admire me). Or me as a ruthless dealer (this from the Swiss critic, now in a wheelchair) who had shattered once and for all the values, if not the pretensions, of the international art market.

Just once, after all this, I caught myself trying to put the Dinner Service, and my inconsequential part in its history, into modest perspective. But it was obvious that 'the Dinner Service' had already been converted from a reality into a phrase. Converted into something arrogant, if not threatening, by the acids of drink.

I had terribly tried to keep it to myself. But it had become, for no reason more subtle than novelty, the toast of the evening. A quietness so English – the plates in my room, at home, still dispersed here and there awaiting me – was being subjected in all ignorance to a lot of French noise.

A jowled man kept raising his glass at me and shaking a clenched fist, as if we alone shared the key. As the guests moved into the flickering dungeon to eat, their interest in 'the Dinner Service' had almost the ebullience of a protest. No concern with me or with what else I had done – no, they had taken over the whole of the Dinner Service, it was magic, and they loved it.

'It is so beautiful,' a slim woman tightly clad in brushed denim was saying, as she sat down and gazed with an erotic sigh at her plate. And I couldn't be sure whether she was referring to the Dinner Service, or the domestic arrangements, or her memory of Willie's last party.

I was aware for the first time of the stirrings of anger.

Anger at a low but deep level, bubbling hungrily in my belly, out of the confusions of teeth, lipstick, eyes, words – all gathering round me in grinning excess to suggest that nothing so valiant, cultured, enlightened as my battle for the Dinner Service had ever happened before. Except of course last night, when they were somewhere else. Or tomorrow, when they would be.

It was at this point, just before a few stalks of asparagus were limply placed in front of us in oily dressing, that Julian Budbury, late, slyly entered the cellar.

I had last seen him in his gallery in London.

We were all seated. He remained standing.

I had been told Budbury might come, was coming, had been delayed, would telephone – and now here he was.

Several voices down the table uttered his first name with glee or mistrust, as if in quotes. Attention wandered from me and focused on him – while he still stood, in a dinner jacket, hands aloft, as if to conduct.

He then made a virtue of apologising at large. Some biographers who sought his opinion had made a special trip. Several guests laughed when he said in a loud aside that biography was the art of murder disguised as resurrection. His *aperçus* had the glitter of having been polished in a hurry on the way to the theatre.

I fingered my plate. It was high time to begin eating – the servants were poised with salvers of the asparagus – but Budbury was allowed to go on, gesticulating, rolling his clever eyes, to tell us that art was what happened when you had nobody to seduce – a peal of merriment from the countess greeted this –

and that masterpieces only came out of their holes when nobody was hunting them. And that produced a quick solitary clap somewhere down the table, probably from the Swiss.

By now I was thinking of bread. Just one mouthful of that crusty bread beyond my reach.

And then Budbury said, 'Now, tell me, who has been getting up this famous tea-set I hear about, I simply must sit next to him or her, because while I must miss nothing I already know about it – which is of course someone's accurate definition (mine, I think) of a critic, even a poor, ill-mannered, revolting old bugger of a critic such as myself.'

As if this were a signal, the servants moved into position with the salvers.

My mouth, watering only a few moments ago, was now quite dry. The anger had begun quivering in my digestive tract. Walvish, with just a hint of irony, led Budbury to the lower end of the table, where I sat in relative state. Flanked by women to whom I now realised I was looking forward to talk.

I was more than ready for a showdown. Indeed there had been a rehearsal already – when Budbury timed his natty little entrance to diminish the Dinner Service as the topic.

I stood up. Shook his clammy hand. And saw in his eyes an exact mirror of the hostility I felt.

'Please, Willie, don't move these charming ladies,' I said. 'It will upset not only the entire table, but me.'

'Ladies never mind,' Budbury said, patting one of their bare shoulders. 'So long as they're in at the kill.'

'Do take that remark a few places away from me,' I said. 'I'd like to see it in the light.'

'Are you shortsighted then? Not good for an expert. Or am I misinformed about your concern for art?'

'However far away you are placed, Mr Budbury, I can see you quite clearly. From my position among these ladies.'

He turned sharply to Walvish, raising his eyes to the vault

with a dramatic groan. 'Place me, dear world,' he said with supreme unction, 'where you will. I have nothing to change but my opinions.'

Then, exploiting the silence created by my own rotten manners, he wickedly added, 'But it would, friends, be awfully nice to sit near this impostor, so that I have at least a dog's chance of altering his views.'

An appreciative titter. Two bits of asparagus descended and curled greenly on my plate.

'Sit the man down,' I said. 'He may not be hungry, but I am. It looks delicious.'

Along the table several hands reached out for bread. Rings flashed. I knew I had lost. I knew also that my failure of temper meant that the Dinner Service, at this function, wouldn't be treated seriously again. I had surrendered it to convulsions of gossip.

For a while I talked with ease to my companions on either side. Their manners deterred them from any direct mention of the Dinner Service. Instead we talked, with proper alternation, of their lives and mine.

One was married to a peach farmer near St Gilles, where the flat country (she came from Paris) would have depressed her, were the bird life not so mysterious. She heard bitterns booming when in the lavatory.

The other (she came from Nîmes) lived in Paris with a banker who spent his working day on the telephone to Switzerland, and we discussed how easy or difficult it was in marriage to conceal the fact that one had a lover.

Whole lives drifted sadly off these two ladies. One blinking at egrets with a daily bewilderment. The other suspicious of a husband too busy with exchange rates to waste afternoons in bed with someone else. Speaking to them, as one course followed another, felt like being married to either.

But throughout these slight intimacies I was aware, just up the table, of Julian Budbury – with a dart at me now and then from his eyes – talking to his neighbours about the Dinner Service.

Fatally I began to listen.

The lady from Nîmes turned to a wizened count called Aristide de Montaren.

The lady from Paris began eating her food with concentration as if roast bird were a substitute for marriage.

With half the table hanging on his words, Budbury was saying, 'Of course I know all about this Dinner Service our friend here is collecting. It happens to be one of the most overrated works of art, if that's the phrase, in Europe. Just the muddle of ugly tableware you would expect, when the best craftsmen that poor old England can provide ruin a good idea by putting it into effect.'

'Bravo,' said an expatriate voice.

'The English,' said Budbury. 'The English – and, remember, I can claim to be more English than most people at this table, so I'm more than aware of their total inadequacy to aesthetic challenge – the English have always hated ideas.'

'Hear, hear,' said the same voice.

'When they get them, which is rare enough, they have to be rushed into intensive care in case they die of shock.' Budbury paused. 'But it's far worse when they act on an idea. For one thing, you see, they can't stand action. They are by nature idle – intended by divine providence for paradise, of course, or so they think, but only if enough gardeners are employed to keep their silly little hedges trimmed.'

Budbury cackled. He could pause at will. He had his audience.

'So, imagine – this great idea, for hundreds of pieces of china, each to be decorated with a pretty picture of their perfectly awful weather or landscape or architecture. And then to be sent across the North Sea – what gross impertinence – to teach the Germans a lesson on how to live and have their being. I mean – you do see?'

Budbury simpered at various flabby allies scraping their plates clean along the table. 'I'm afraid,' he said, 'that this is the conclusion all civilised countries reached long ago – that your Englishman must be kept away from art at all costs. Pension him off if you will, give him a garden to fill with vulgar blooms out of packets, allow him now and then to patronise the rest of Europe by pretending he has defended its freedom by playing cricket – but don't let him within a mile of any such refined concept as a work of art.'

'He's right,' said someone sepulchrally.

'If he doesn't think he made the work of art,' Budbury said, 'he'll think it was made for him. Or, if not that, then it was designed by foreigners to cheat him – or make him feel small. But then, of course, friends, he *is* small.'

Budbury glanced at me. 'Not in stature, or in his opinion of himself, or in ambition, or in his unshakeable view that only his view of a matter is correct – but small in his mind, in his heart. Each Englishman is a vacuum in which no idea can breathe, each a desert in which the great trees of art and life find nowhere to root.'

Budbury gazed down at me with a flat mischievous smile. 'Don't you agree? Surely you must. You look English enough. Or perhaps, if my view is right, you have no idea what I'm talking about?'

'No,' I said.

'Be clear,' he said wolfishly. 'You do agree? You do look English? Or you do have no idea?'

Knowing the effort useless – but suspecting I could win back the loyalty of at least some part of his audience – yet realising that audience was not worth having because all it wanted was a fight or sudden illness or someone to jump in a fountain – I did steadily feel that I owed it to the Dinner Service to put up a reasonable defence.

Such a defence would sound pompous and say nothing and discount me as humourless.

I couldn't rival his colossal cheek, but I had put my heart into the Dinner Service. Awaiting me at home were pieces for which I had sacrificed comfort, morality and sense. It was there, there, far more centrally than Budbury. With a past no less solid than this cellar centuries old. With a present far more alive than this party's hollow vivacity. But above all I believed in it.

I had no opinion about it. I did not take this or that particular view of it. Indeed I had no will or reason even to discuss it. But the Dinner Service was being attacked, and I felt the surges of anger which might naturally arise in a man whose only child was threatened.

I looked with an attempted smile at Budbury. No eloquence came to my rescue.

'No,' I said.

'No what?'

'Just no,' I said.

'You can't just say no, unless perhaps you're English?' Budbury said, as if shielding his audience from anticlimax. 'Why, I mean, it's simply a way of agreeing with me – without having to surrender your stupid principles in public.'

Was he blustering on purpose? To gain yet more sympathy?

I noted in the eye of the lady from Nîmes her sense that I was on the run. The look was of pity. The lady from Paris had kindly waited a bit too long for me to launch a remark of devastating finality. No such remark sprang to mind.

The trouble was I wanted both to defend the Dinner Service and to keep it to myself. The two impulses were not to be reconciled.

'No,' I repeated with a shrug.

'Like English art, this self-appointed defender of the faith has but one word to his name,' Budbury said at large. 'It is a negative word. The word is no. I rest my case.'

His podgy hands bumped down on the table edge. A fat finger tapped a plate. A few tentative Arabs slid from the shadows with a view to serving strawberries. The incident was almost at an end.

'Willie,' Budbury said loudly, 'I shan't be dining here again, old boy. You can't get a decent chinwag with anyone. Chaps clam up, d'you know.'

A shudder of rage assailed me. To improve his joke Budbury stood up, patted his mouth with a napkin and pretended to start leaving.

I knew that the grimace of insult on his face was manufactured to garnish the occasion. I even knew that he meant hardly a word, whereas every syllable I had been careful not to utter was exactly what I had meant. Equally I was sure that if I said or did nothing Budbury would sit down, wolf strawberries with cream dripping in triumph off his lips, and ignore both me and the Dinner Service for the rest of the evening. He would have had his fun.

So I could scarcely leave it at that. Nothing, on the other hand, entered my mind to say. Words were Budbury's empty province. He had used a lot of them. They were little fat fists that pounded an ugly tattoo on my memory. They had seduced by violence a body of uncertain people who only wanted to live better or differently. Who had mutely asked me, or anyone else, to say more than no. Who were seeking in these cellars a less trivial kind of party.

I had only seconds to decide on a course of action, as Budbury stood in blatant mockery of his own discourse, mouth pinched in, his entire life writing off mine.

Fire inflamed my veins, my resolve. There seemed only one way of altering the immediate future to accommodate the monstrosity of the man.

I didn't question it. I was hardly even aware that it was happening. I stepped up to him and slapped his back hard, to alert him to violence, so that he staggered against his chair. Grasped one lapel which swung him round, a bit pop-eyed, to face me. Then with unthinking satisfaction landed a deep thudding punch in the stomach where all that meat and asparagus was churning amid wine. Then tripped him at the ankle so that his big body sliced sideways against the table and his reading specs flew off into a bowl of cream. And finally, warming to my subject, my strength feeding with rigour on a diet of rage, put my fist firmly, not too hard, but with an impact that squelched and hurt my knuckles, into the flat of his face.

Budbury dithered to the floor, where on a rug he began moaning. Even that was theatrical, as if he had rehearsed for the assault.

'No,' I said very loudly indeed.

There was no other word to convey my message and none at all to excuse my action. The responsibility, the relief from anger, began to suffuse my arteries in waves of pleasure. I had snatched the Dinner Service back, if only for myself, in the nick of time.

An Arab stood by, so shocked that strawberries were tipping in a trickle from the dish in his hands. I withdrew a pace, seeing not clearly. I heard Walvish, my host, hurrying to the scene of the crime, over which candlelight flickered in a spasm of melodrama.

I knew that in the course of the evening, when the final balance was drawn, Budbury had committed far more violence than I. But at least I had performed the current equivalent of dancing in the fountain or having a seizure in public. Talk would flourish.

Some toady was wiping cream off the sod's glasses. I was just thinking it might be wise to retire when a man to whom I hadn't talked, the small grey amused aristocrat called Aristide de Montaren, sidled up to me with an almost lascivious air of conspiracy and murmured, 'You have struck, sir, a great blow for society.'

And suddenly it sounded against all the evidence as though the Dinner Service might be remembered for a long time to come.

* * *

Flight. Packing fast. Note of apology to Walvish. Dinner Service wrapped in dirty shirts. Ring for taxi. Night train from Avignon to Paris. Day boat from Calais to Dover. An hour at the club to stow my valuables. Call to Sophie. Sophie out. Taxi to Heathrow.

And Iceland at last!

The airport bus took me through miles of crumpled lava that seemed only just to have cooled. Nothing green in sight, except faint starts of moss on the rock.

Reykjavik's small but grandest hotel, a glimpse of the last century, stood in a tiny square containing edifices of rough pumice and chunky oxblood stone. A toytown city only inches thick – behind a handful of heavy façades stretched a waste-land of wooden huts. Small factories. Curving lines of bungalows perched impermanently on the ashy slopes.

On every corner of the diminutive centre small boys cried out the rival claims of thin tabloids. A penetrating sleet fell. Even the banks had a cosy air – only the prices in the shops looked huge. The air stank of cod-liver oil and goaty petrol.

The fun started the moment I signed my name in the register.

Ah, said the girl. An old painter in the dining-room liked visitors from abroad and knew everyone, since everyone did know everyone in Iceland.

The artist was noisily consuming cheroots and newspapers and lamb stew under the bad light of a chandelier. His face was rough, he hadn't shaved, he had spent the day packing fish. The herring had come in.

Oh, yes, of course he remembered Maurice Bone. His very name was legend, a footnote to the sagas. The man I needed to meet was an importer of spare parts. Whose offices one could see from the hotel window.

The girl was dispatched as a messenger. From the street the cries of boys were edged with urgency. Umbrellas jostled on the narrow pavement. And here now was Sigurdur, trim, sharp-eyed, ebullient, clasping my hands as he offered every possible service to the friend of a friend.

Yes, of course he remembered Maurice Bone. Who so loved women, talk, drink. Who sat up deep into the night, coming out to fish in the dawn, cut hay, service cars, teach in school.

But the man who knew him best was a Minister, to be located in the Parliament across the street. Where we must now with all urgency go to find him – unless he was at the National Theatre, two streets away, left and left again – or editing his newspaper. Or perhaps, since the herring had come in, also fishing.

The sleet iced into our eyes as the three of us, accompanied by the receptionist in case her services were needed, trotted from one grandiose but tiny building to the next in quest of the Minister.

His name was Dagfinnur. He was always one step ahead. Sigurdur kept expecting to meet him in the jerky ballet of umbrellas along the pavement. The painter knew exactly where he was, but had forgotten. We all huddled together, chatting it over. The quicksilver of the sleet blurred the intimate horizons of the town. Then turned sharply to rain, which fell in a short burst. Then stopped.

Why was everyone so excited? I felt at home.

Then there he was – Dagfinnur. Standing on springy legs in his office, a lank figure with a thin florid face and tawny hair on top. In his hands were papers of state.

These, at the mention of Bone's name, he dropped in a muddle on his desk – while in a metallic tenor, in slow English as if carving runes, he drew a word-picture – he was also a noted poet – of his old hero, the Englishman who had come to these heights of Europe to live and die – a good man, a brave man, a simple man. Who understood the brutal necessity in Iceland for every member of society to pull his weight for the common good, whether making hay, servicing cars, fishing when the herring was in, teaching, directing plays, being an elected representative, writing poems, or selling newspapers on the corner of the street. Or preferably all eight activities at once.

With a modest bow the Minister said that tomorrow, when he wasn't busy, he would take me to Bone's grave, if there was a plane – for it was 200 miles away from Reykjavik and 50 weeks of the year inaccessible by road. By this time the spare-parts man and the painter had melted away with the sleet. No doubt to serve others with their manifold skills.

Next morning I felt I had come to the end of my search. Certainly I could go no further.

We flew alone in a fifty-seater. Occasional gaps in racing cloud revealed the black haunch of a mountain of jasper sand. A ruby-red cliff that sloped down to the ultramarine of a glacier. Then acres of gun-metal land ribbed by flows of dead lava – or torrents of white water that looked silently dreadful from the air.

No human sign was visible. Except at the edges, and then not often, there was nothing on this waste of an island except abstracts of vividly sad colour that ended in the lash of the sea.

Our aircraft bumbled endlessly along the coastline at no great height, seabirds angling below us in flocks, until with a warning roar we swooped bumpily towards the waves – and then were whizzing down a long beach, the sea frothing on one side, a fringe of scrub arising on the other towards the bulk of a glacier.

The aircraft, though a scheduled flight, would wait until we were ready to return. We drove in a truck down the beach for a mile or two, wheels spitting pebbles off the track. And then saw, tucked into the steep wet hill where sheep grazed, the farmstead where Maurice Bone had spent his last days.

The farmer had been told by telephone what I wanted. Few words were exchanged. None understood by me.

Leaving me space, Dagfinnur passed amiably into a preoccupation of his own – he sat at the farmer's table reading a heavily bound Bible.

The wife took a scared look at me. Then softly closed the kitchen door behind her.

The farmer unlatched a back room and stood aside with eyes averted.

A distended cobweb floated between jamb and lintel.

A sweet fatty smell of mutton stuck for a moment in my gullet, Dagfinnur turned a page, then I walked into the back room. The latch clicked.

It was to enter a cell. Twelve feet square – and overlooking a bank of frowsty grass that cut out most of the light. A narrow bed, a table nailed out of driftwood, a stained bench, a damp bulging curtain with clothes behind it. Under the bed was a battered utility suitcase from the war, light blue, with tinny corners.

The only other decoration, which was on the wall, looked more like a window than the real one.

It was a plate at least 24 inches long and over half as wide – probably one of the grander serving-dishes – and its intense whiteness cast into the room an opalescence that suggested it was the only source of light. King's College, Cambridge, as expected. In this silence I could almost hear the emotive distance of four-part harmony on the air. Or a voice intoning sacred words into the random acoustics of that masterpiece.

I stared at it for a long time. One or two hurrying academics pursued their traditions across the court. I sensed the immediacy of the secret they had just discovered – the missing phrase in an otherwise perfect text – the next scientific step towards either making the world fit to live in or exploding it. Their gowns flew in the wind. The high verticals of the chapel outlined a declaration of the ideal. The buttressed bays were as measured as pentameters. The pointed windows concealed just as much as this window into another man's lifetime.

For this was Bone's bedroom. He had died in it. But his things were still here. I knew that he had travelled far. I suspected he was searching for something hard to find because it had no obvious outward existence. I imagined that he might have thought that working on the land, near the sea, at the remotest point possible in his own continent, was the answer – or one of the answers – to some question which he didn't quite know how to pose.

And all he had to remind him of home was a bit of a university on the wall.

But why had he chosen so to honour a tradition with which he had no personal link? To him that dish could only be a building, if rather a good one. Perhaps it was also a history. Was that it?

Did Maurice Bone, finding an unlikely utopia on this coast cut off except for an annual fortnight from all the places and values he might be expected to hold dear, suffering the weather, the edge of poverty, a forbidding biblical silence, did he still need the idea that his roots mattered enough to look at them every day as if they were a window?

Or did he just think that life – as sung in that choir, or splitting atoms or hairs or differences in labs and common rooms, or writing angelic books with a devilish gusto – might have turned out more splendidly for him, if only he had been granted such different choices?

I had to know. The room had been kept just as he left it – any clues? I couldn't ask anyone else. They wouldn't grasp the level on which I was risking my questions. I took my eyes off that dense allusive window on England. And began to look round the room with a rising sense that I had lived here myself.

I had very few possessions. I had deliberately offloaded them as I was drawn towards isolation of this kind. I wanted nothing more. Ever again. A few clothes to wear – push them away behind a curtain – but why a suitcase?

No intention of packing up, leaving, trying somewhere else. But what if I wanted to write of my experience, if only to make it real? To have a mirror facing me on paper? Then I might imagine that tatty suitcase to be my study, my concealed narcissism, which I would draw out from under the bed when everyone else was asleep.

I drew it out. The catches snapped up. It was almost falling to pieces.

But inside was a cheap notebook. Bought here in Iceland. Packed to within a few pages of the end with writing in pencil.

I sat on the bed reading it, now and then lifting my glance to a summer morning in Cambridge or the windy grasses of an almost uninhabited corner of Iceland. I read both the lines and between them. And there was nothing.

The notebook was not illiterate, just feeble. Bone gassed on lamely. He bothered over his health in an ungainly hand. He boasted about the hours he had worked for how little praise, and the lack of sleep, and the dreadful food.

A man emerged, but not a specially nice one. At least not one given to expressing intelligent thought in prose that searched the heart. I had hoped to find my own answers writ large. Or simply writ. It was a profound disappointment to me. And Cambridge still hung gleaming on the wall – just as a polite knuckle tapped at the door.

We were to have a meal before flying back. The thickly built woman who had looked after Maurice Bone placed on the table a dish of warmed lamb in chunks, off which a tacky membrane was peeling. It smelt feral. Large waxen potatoes with woolly edges came separately in a covered bowl. She withdrew.

Dagfinnur looked at me wryly, then pulled a flat flask of whisky from an inner pocket. In a mime of instruction, eyes on me, he took a bite of the untoothsome meat, half chewed it. Then soaked it in a swig of spirit before rushing it past his gullet.

Then he handed me the flask. We sat in silence consuming the fringes of the repast, now and then gagging courteously. The fat that riddled the mutton in thick seams clove to the palate. Only the whisky fired it past my defences.

'I have told them,' he said quietly, 'that you will take his property back to England. Out of respect and perhaps love they have kept his room for many years as he left it, but they are still sleeping in the kitchen and I know you will bring them relief.'

The farmer had packed the wartime suitcase while we lunched. All Bone's belongings, including the dish, fitted into it. We made our farewells – my gratitude inexpressible, theirs seemingly deeper. And as we began walking, against the wind, across that beach, towards the distant aircraft, I said, 'What did he see in it?'

'Ask yourself the same question,' Dagfinnur said.

'Yes, I do, all the time – but why did a man who travelled light burden himself with a heavy picture of a place that apparently meant nothing to him?'

'Here you are carrying the same heavy picture along the same empty beach.'

I looked up. The wind whipped tears out of my eyes. Far away a commotion – round the ladder at the aircraft's rear exit. I had a nightmarish vision of a queue of sheep jostling for entry.

'Yes, but I have others. I have lots of places. I've collected them from all over the continent.'

'But what do you see in them?' Dagfinnur said.

'In a lot of pieces I suppose I see peace and order. Then there's a gently expressed emotion – what to call it? An affection – that's more noticeable in some than in others. Depending on who the original artist was – they were done by different people, you know.'

'I see.'

'There's usually a fine balance too.'

'Ah,' he said.

Surely that was a ewe highstepping up the ladder. I must be mistaken. The light was deceptive. Darkened by low cloud buffeting over the beach.

'And in most of them – or is this imagination, I wonder? – there's a sense of a life that hasn't yet quite gone, despite all the differences between now and the time they were manufactured – in or around 1914 – and the pieces make that life intensely familiar to me. I want to preserve what is best in that time without being dominated by it.'

'Wasn't Maurice on the look-out for these things also?' Dagfinnur said. 'He came here to seek the opposite of peace and order – Iceland is never safe, we are on a geological fault – but perhaps he wished to be reminded of them.'

Was this true? King's was only one piece out of many. Could it be enough to contain in an epigram the pattern of his values? Blinking into the distance, I decided against my better judgment that sheep were indeed being introduced into the body of the aircraft. Terns overhead arrowed out towards the shoreline.

'And the point that really touches me,' I said, 'is that all these views and visions add up to an elaborately complete statement made with infinite care, despite the fragility of the material.'

'Yes, and this material comes from the earth – perhaps under our feet, as we walk here?'

Dagfinnur was somehow doing his best to clarify. But interfering with a train of thought that more and more led nowhere.

Always – at the most promising moment – a distraction reared. Now it was those sheep. A figure hunched in gleaming waterproofs under the tailplane was prodding a bunch of ewes with a stick into the aircraft. Dagfinnur stood back, as though waiting for the first-class to precede us.

'And then,' I said, 'the Service is all the richer for my accumulated knowledge of it. I've grown up with what those pictures are saying – and now they seem to have changed me. How? No idea. But that wouldn't account for a man stubbornly bringing a piece of it, with all the risks of breakage and loss, all the way here to the end of the world.'

'And you have come here to find it. Is not that also stubborn?'

As the last sheep was bullied up the ladder, the engines began grudgingly to mutter – the propellers jerked once or twice – the tone lifted. Dagfinnur raised his voice to a shout.

'The answer to why he did it is not in my power to give. Perhaps not in yours either. Why do you not just accept that Maurice took this course – as you have – and so enjoy a mystery for yourself? I learn in politics that not everything has to have a solution.'

'But it helps.'

'It only helps if people believe there is one.'

We entered the plane. All the seats but three had been detached, stacked against the inner fuselage, to allow room for the sheep. They stood massed in the cabin. Heads trembling above a sea of wool, gazing at us through slits of incurious fear – an occasional bleat sounding almost human above the roar of take-off.

I reflected on this their last journey. Destined first for the slaughter-house, they were soon to be swallowed in viscous chunks by families wearing sweaters spun from their ancestors. It never occurred to me that from such macabre speculation any lesson was to be learnt.

I fell into a doze.

After a time Dagfinnur said abruptly, 'There she is – look!' I strained across him to the window, striving to recall a noisy dream.

Down below, far to the right, the dark cone of a mountain was spilling, upwards into the air, turbulent thrusts of steam in which tiny prickles of fire burnt into the eye. Over it hung miles of smoke shredded by the wind.

'Hekla,' said Dagfinnur with pride.

The volcano must have been active beneath the clouds on our earlier flight. For now I could see steady glinting streams of movement down the skirts of the mountain, the dully bronze lava sizzling unheard as it hit the river, puffing more steam into the atmosphere. A ewe muttered behind us.

'It is always changing here,' Dagfinnur said, as we passed once more into cloud. 'We have not tamed the world yet. We can all be killed tomorrow, so it is that much more worth being alive. Perhaps that is why people come to Iceland and stay here. It is not a place for anyone who likes his past too much.'

'Or his future,' I said.

The engine note changed. Preparing for descent.

'How did he die?'

Hooves scraped wildly on aluminium. The slight shift downwards upset the sheep into a chorus of bleats. My safety belt was tight.

'He died very happy,' Dagfinnur said. 'He was the man he wished to be in the place where he wanted to live. You wish the details?'

'No,' I said. An intuition, irrational: that whatever had happened to the man whose suitcase was in my keeping must be my fate too. Sacrificing my health and strength, possibly, in a last bid to master the implications of the Dinner Service.

'In fact he had a heart attack,' Dagfinnur said.

And now we were landing.

I had all I wanted. I possessed the final piece. The one piece that nobody else's resources could have run to earth. The sheep were herded out by men in sheepskin aprons. I had no desire to leave – yet I had to advertise my triumph. There was no point in owning so obvious and unique a key to England unless I made something of it. Proved to the universe that I alone had achieved this miracle. Proved to myself that I was of similar worth.

At the hotel Dagfinnur left me swiftly. The herring were still in. The government was in crisis. He had students to teach. Or a poem in mind.

The little square had an air of permanence, as if painted. Etched on a plate.

On reaching Boxer Street SW8, the first task was to lay out the Dinner Service where I could see it. And show it to Sophie.

An hour alone – she was still at work – passed as swiftly as that first evening when I repaired the church at West Dole. Hot and bothered, I scurried about the living-room positioning plates, dishes and platters wherever Sophie had left a space. In a constantly changing pattern. According to no aesthetic theory, but sheer whim. So – a busy montage of England unloaded from boxes, stripped of their paper, wiped by a hand, then propped not at all safely while I made a judgment. No – or so-so – or an inch to the left – or absolutely spot-on. Or leave it till later.

A few near misses. The Brecon Beacons started rolling off a chair and I scooped them into my hand. Yet the risk of breakage was far less serious than failing to pose this exhibition of myself and my doings in time for Sophie's arrival.

She of all people must see – would see – the beauty of the many strands which I had woven together into a sort of whole from many separate places. Here they all were at last, at home, under one roof, coordinating all our associations, our scraps of past, which hitherto had been scattered abroad.

Possibly they also took matters a little further than we could – if left to ourselves – simply because they were no metaphor. No symbol for anything. But only an interlocking series of splendid objects that added up to more than we could ask for.

Sophie arrived home, not expecting me.

We dithered in the hall kissing each other. Her warmth was commendable for someone surprised.

'Oh, a man came,' she said.

'What man?'

'Some German from Leicester or somewhere. He said you'd given him some money for his plates – so he was delivering them.'

'Where are they?'

'Heavens, there's plenty of time for all that. Let's go in and talk. All this time with no one to mix me a decent screwdriver – darling. I'm parched.'

Sophie entered the living-room.

'Oh,' she said.

She heaved a sigh. Then slowly, in the manner of royalty, moved here and there with a short-sighted smile. Saying not a word. Her hands fluttering a brief acknowledgment over this or that view which she recognised – her eyes concentrating for a second on a landmark, a group of trees, a detail.

'I shall have to look at it again,' she said. 'It's very confusing to take it in all at once.'

She moved to the Black Country. Then away to the Western Isles. Her glance darted off to the hollow magnificence of Tintern Abbey. Above which on a poetic slope we had once picnicked.

Then she said, 'I hadn't quite realised it was all so cosy. Doesn't that mean it's not art?'

'It doesn't have to mean anything,' I said. 'Can't some things just be themselves? This happens to be here and now – in all this mess. That's all that matters.'

She paused over half Bournemouth, which had come from a Paris music-hall, via an ex-lover of hers.

'Where's the rest?' she said.

And then Maiden Newton. A prehistoric tump. We made love on it.

'Oh, darling, of course it's not art, is it?' she said. 'It's not good enough – it's far too much like life.'

'What exactly are you insulting?'

'Certainly not you. Not the Dinner Service either. Nothing in fact,' Sophie said with a surprised air. 'I only know that I'm touched by the whole thing – don't ask me why – because you got it together, and it's far older than either of us. And yet it makes me feel young. I keep seeing places that look the same as they used to, and they're still there, and I long to go to them again because I shall see them quite differently.'

For the first time she reached out a finger to touch the surface of a plate. Just the rim. Her nail moved over a curve of vine-leaves and stopped short at the eagle. It was of Cheltenham. It must have been lent me by Bodo Zinzendorf. Or given.

I had hardly looked at it. But I felt – with pleasure – that Sophie was seeing more than I would. Meanwhile she uttered a brief screech and said, 'I've got it, darling! The whole thing's just our childhoods imagined all over again – lots of stuff we were told in the nursery about England, and only believed because we were silly. And it's now turning out to be real! Myth isn't in it. Legends don't quite make the point either. It's more. Not much more, but a bit more. Do you see that?'

'Yes.'

If prompted, I could see anything. That was the point.

'Just look at that ghastly pretentious house that's so much a part of us that we automatically say how beautiful.'

She was jabbing a finger at the front of Chatsworth, where servants were unloading baggage from a carriage.

'All I can see,' Sophie said vehemently, 'is a bunny rabbit running across that lawn. Soon it'll vanish down a hole – and then life starts. Look at those poor servants. They're not noticing a thing.'

Less regal now, Sophie. Tentative. Dropping the resistance with which she had entered the living-room. And moving on to the view of Salisbury which I had exhumed in Cornwall and bought from that nice potter.

'Look!' she cried. Her body bent desirably over the cathedral close. 'I bet that's a satyr behind that tree. Any minute he'll jump out and rape the entire chapter to the accompaniment of a mass by Byrd or someone, and all we can do is remember from guide-books how great it was they used Purbeck marble for the pillars. Isn't that pathetic? But honestly can't you see that randy little faun? He's one of us.'

'Do you mean this, Sophie, in a literal way?'

What a boring response. She drew back, her dress falling into folds around her hips. She stared at my eyes with a slight frown – as if I had deliberately misunderstood the whole matter.

'My goodness,' she said. 'This is exciting.'

Well, yes. In her own way she was getting the message. That

the Dinner Service, like everything else we looked at properly, had its own narrative – which must and would take it further, and take us further with it. Not for long could it maintain the perfection it had hastily achieved in these ramshackle surroundings. It was only a moment – but I had all the entertainment I would ever need. My whole life gathered from the corners of memory into one place, one time, with the one person who had most shared them. And there was more. Always there was more.

This was exciting.

Sophie then said, 'Of course I don't think one would want to eat off it. I wouldn't dare – and also it's a bit shop-soiled. As they say, you never know where it's been.'

'I could tell you.'

'And I absolutely don't want to put it on the wall – you know, like all those suburban ducks. Or into a glass cabinet, and then someone would lose the key.'

Was the girl taking over the Dinner Service, for heaven's sake? And, if so, why?

'No,' she went on, 'I prefer the pictures in my own mind. Just propped up any old how against the sides of it, where they've always been. Nor can you sell them really.'

'Why not? They'd bring in . . .'

'Oh, they're far too valuable to sell. You'd start niggling and bargaining – you'd lose friends and influence no one – you'd lie awake cursing yourself for having the money but not enough of it. And then slowly but surely, for profit, not for love, the whole doings would be scattered all over the place again and end up in all sorts of wrong hands. That would hardly do. And you can't hide it.'

'We could keep it to ourselves for a while.'

'That's awfully dim,' Sophie said. 'It's like never wearing your jewellery in case you get mugged. Don't you want to show it off? It's you, darling. The last thing I want is to keep you to myself. You're my hero – you've done it. I shall be showing you off to everyone. How could I possibly deny other people such pots of pleasure? It might stop them boring me.'

'That leaves only one alternative.'

'Such as, poppet?'

'Break it,' I mildly suggested.

'Break it? All of it?'

'Could be fun. Think, we'd be free of the bloody thing. We've already got the best out of it – me collecting it up – you just seeing it all this once – both of us recognising with a gasp how incredibly beautiful it is.'

'Are you serious? No, you're not serious.'

No, her trouble was that she was being rather too serious. And at that moment my suspicion of Sophie quickened. What did she really want? At whose behest? If she couldn't make a noble joke of our possession, my instinct was to hit out.

Then she said calmly, 'You taught me – it's your fault, this, and it's why I'm here and not in bed with your stupid rival – you taught me, darling, that unless you've got a better idea nothing should ever be destroyed, because it's the things you keep and guard and love that give you the better idea.'

She gazed at me on the brink of tears – then away to the white circles and oblongs of the dishes. 'I've fallen in love with your wretched Dinner Service, so you can jolly well go and do what you like with it.'

She walked towards the kitchen. Stamping out, as usual, precisely when something of note was on the point of utterance.

Then Sophie returned, hands behind her back.

'I've one thing to add,' she said, 'before you hammer it all to bits.'

She now gave me a lecture. I hadn't obviously been reading her column. She said that National Arts (or Ranston for short) had assembled from foreign museums, or twisted the arms of private owners to extort, or appealed to friendly governments for the loan of, slightly more than half of the Dinner Service as manufactured in 1914. Say five hundred pieces in all. And that these were safely in the hands of the authorities and not open to offer. That they were, thanks partly to Sophie's support in her newspaper, to be put on public exhibition during the summer – as arguably the last great work of art, or what remained of it, created in England before the outbreak of a war that destroyed, if not art itself, at least the chance of any similarly luxurious manifestation of its powers – depending as this did on the efforts of workers poorly paid. And that His Royal Highness had graciously agreed to open the Exhibition by attending a private view well in advance of the public. In his own house.

'His own house?'

'Yes,' Sophie said. 'He has bought a house in Dorset.'

This house seemed of importance to Sophie. She was blinking at me expectantly.

'So what sort of house?' I said. 'Is it a secret?'

'The sort of house, darling, that invariably starts off a search for the Imperial German Dinner Service, you goon,' Sophie said. 'This sort of house.'

And as if humouring a child she whizzed her hands from behind her back. And held the plate in front of her chest, image towards me. And of course I recognised it at once.

It was the plate she had found with the sovereigns under the floorboards of poor old Fentiman's cottage which she had bought for too little money to keep him alive in his dotage. End of surprise.

It was a touchingly English sort of image, one of the best. Enclosed in the usual pattern – vine-leaves, the eagle – the Prince's new house occupied the centre of the plate. A home. Lots of nice families had lived there, adding on, suffering outbreaks of fire, surviving, demolishing chapels or wings, for well over half a dozen centuries. Longer if you counted the foundations of the earlier house – there was always an earlier house – that first overlooked the Dorset hills towards the glimmer of the sea.

I saw the thickets where children played at building worlds of their own. And octets of windows behind which generations dined in quarrel and peace. And memories of parties that burst out on to that lawn. And kisses behind the rhododendrons that banked the fringes of the image. And dances.

In the contours of that house I saw pain, jealousy, waves of itinerant happiness, amusement, horror – and, worst, familiarity. In the search for its likenesses I had felt almost all of that. And now I felt it again. The only thing I could do now was ask Sophie, and I asked it, the obvious question – whether this was the first piece of the Dinner Service (just as my own baptism had been our church at West Dole) which HRH had been shown.

It wasn't worth asking. My chest irrelevantly hurt.

'Yes,' she said. 'Why otherwise would he have been interested?'

To which there was no answer.

Except one.

'Don't you know why I went out to look for the Dinner Service, Sophie? Here's just one clue. It's not the only point, of course. But I did it because nobody does it. No one tries any more. Well, they don't know about love. It's out of fashion to go roaring off on a chase which you can only win if the opposition goes soft. Or is stupid enough to let you. It's what every little boy used to want to do. After reading Buchan under the bedclothes. After following all the heroes into hair's-breadth escapes from violence, dishonesty, power – all the things none of us likes even when we're grown up. And I did it because it's in us all to do it – perhaps we get only one chance, and I wasn't going to pass mine up. And now I look in the mirror and it says I'm younger – but I'm not, that's what's wonderful. I'm more grown up. And also I'm still the child who doesn't want or need to do it again. Have you done it, Sophie? Or are you happy just to write about other people doing it?'

'I haven't done it,' Sophie said. 'But all the same I love you.'

'Because I don't want these plates any more?'

'Because I want you.'

End of story.

Well, not quite.

The evening before the banquet – a July night clearing after a showery afternoon – His Royal Highness gave a party at his new home. Largely for the benefit of the media – whose interest in the mysteries of our culture Sophie had aroused in her column by frequent mention of the Dinner Service.

This was to be unveiled by Courtney Ranston at 10 p.m.

The gardens were adrift with people as we arrived. Most of them I didn't know – despite invitations sent out all over Europe to anyone who had helped me. Whatever I might have said in passion, I hadn't in truth done it alone.

Figures preying on the Dinner Service – they hadn't even viewed it yet – shifted in and out of the several bars in black ties. Cars debouching half-recognised people from London were spirited away to the stable yards as soon as the high heels had stepped out. Owls hooted behind the cries of greeting.

I'd had enough by then.

I didn't want to hit Julian Budbury again. Or see Guin. Or face up to Anton Moritz – to whose sister out of guilt I had paid a ludicrous sum.

Philippe Guin, if here, would only be trying to make love to Sophie. Or Desmond Turvey would. Yes, Turvey. He would ask me what I was doing here.

And Bodo Zinzendorf would find some way of placing me under an obligation. Even if Moritz didn't.

And then there was the way Courtney Ranston might patronise me. By referring in his speech – too long by half – to the ultimate generosity of one man who had made over to the public his haul of close on fifty pieces of the Dinner Service.

Or by gloating in private over his affair with Sophie, which nobody knew was over.

And Sophie too was a risk. She might, with all that champagne, vanish behind the rhododendrons. With Guin. Or Turvey or Ranston.

Worst of all I might, in drink, start wondering what to do next.

Or anything might happen.

Original Fiction in Paladin

Paper Thin £2.95 ☐
Philip First
From the author of THE GREAT PERVADER: a wonderfully original collection of stories about madness, love, passion, violence, sex and humour.

Don Quixote £2.95 ☐
Kathy Acker
From the author of BLOOD AND GUTS IN HIGH SCHOOL: a visionary collage–novel in which Don Quixote is a woman on an intractable quest; a late twentieth-century LEVIATHAN; a stingingly powerful and definitely unique novel.

To order direct from the publisher just tick the titles you want and fill in the order form.